This
Means

WAR

This
Means
WAR

Paul Hollis, Ph.D.
Claire Hollis, Ph.D.

Warfare Publications

This Means War!

ISBN 0-9673122-0-5

Library of Congress Catalog Card Number: 99-96603

Copyright © 1999 by Warfare Publications

Printed in the United States of America

Published by: Warfare Publications
                  PMB #206
                  4577 Gunn Highway
                  Tampa, FL 33624 USA
                  (813) 935-4673
                  Fax: (813) 935-2387
                  E-mail: WarfareP@aol.com
                  Web site: www.warfareplus.com

Cover Design: Brenda Belliveau

Unless otherwise indicated, all scripture references are from the authorized *King James Version* of the Bible.

There was war in heaven
and the devil was cast out.

Now there is war on earth
and it's being waged against mankind.

Be a warrior!

Be a winner!

The victory celebration is coming soon
and it will be worth it all!

**THIS BOOK BRINGS THE WAR
TO THE ENEMY!**

Table of Contents

ACKNOWLEDGEMENTS

Special thanks to Deborah Murphy and Carol Russell for spending so much time and effort wading through and typing my messy notes.

Thanks to our editor, Carol B. Patterson.

DEDICATION

This book is dedicated to the Lord Jesus Christ Who gave all the information and knowledge on the following pages. He is "The Deliverer." He has already won the war—we are only His mouthpiece!

FOREWORD

By Deborah Murphy

Paul and Claire Hollis are called into deliverance ministry and have declared war on satan's kingdom. Sadly, there are thousands, perhaps millions, of wounded, battered Christians who don't even know they are in a battle. If you don't know you're in a battle, how can you discern and understand your enemy—and how can you receive victory?

The Word of God says, *My people are destroyed for lack of knowledge (Hosea 4:6).* There is a desperate need for God's people to know that they have been given the keys to the kingdom, but they also need to know how to use them.

Paul and Claire have a calling to teach the church how to:

    a. Identify their enemy
    b. Learn his tactics
    c. Successfully use their weapons of warfare

Their goal is to:

    a. Set captives free through deliverance
    b. Unite the body of Christ
    c. Tear down the devil's kingdom

The average church today is not teaching spiritual warfare in-depth; in fact, some don't even touch on this much-needed subject at all. That is where Paul and Claire's ministry comes in. The front line has become their new home and they are anointed for deliverance. They see a person's need to be whole in spirit, soul and body and they devote themselves to equipping Christians with their weapons of warfare— accompanied by the garment of praise!

INTRODUCTION

NOTE: The purpose of this book is to expose and expel satan and, while he is one of the "centerpieces" of the book, we do not wish to honor him in any way. For this reason, his name will be treated as a common noun and will not be capitalized in this manuscript. We consider him "lower case" and, even at the risk of being criticized for being grammatically incorrect, we will follow this procedure.

This book will explain to you how a demonic influence can come into your life, show you how to get rid of it, and how to keep it from coming back.

Demons need bodies to live in because that is how they fulfill their mission, but God did not create humans to be the dwelling place for devils. He created humans to love and praise Him! He could have designed us to be like puppets so that He could pull our strings and force us to praise Him, but He chose not to do it that way. Instead, He made us with a **free will so that we could choose whom we would serve**.

In the following pages, you will gain enough information to declare war on satan and his demonic kingdom and WIN, and in doing this, become totally free to serve your CREATOR without hindrance.

The testimonies recorded herein are true accounts of people who have gone through our deliverance program. Their names, descriptions, and in some instances, even genders, have been changed to protect their privacy.

1

What Christ Said About Deliverance

What Christ Said About Deliverance

A nd he said unto them, Go ye into all the world, and preach the gospel to every creature. (16) He that believeth and is baptized shall be saved; but he that believeth not shall be damned. (17) And these signs shall follow them that believe; In my name shall they cast out devils; they shall speak with new tongues; (18) They shall take up serpents; and if they drink any deadly thing, it shall not hurt them; they shall lay hands on the sick, and they shall recover. (Mark 16:15-18)

These were the last words that Jesus spoke before He ascended into heaven. This is called "The Great Commission" and was given to us, the Body of Christ.

Jesus also had another Great Commission and it is found in Luke 4:18:

The Spirit of the Lord is upon me, because he hath anointed me to preach the gospel to the poor (evangelism); *he hath sent me to heal the brokenhearted* (healing and deliverance), *to preach deliverance to the captives* (deliverance), *and recovering of sight to the blind* (healing), *to set at liberty them that are bruised* (deliverance).

This call of God was acknowledged at the beginning of His ministry. This Great Commission was first prophesied in the Old Testament by Isaiah, a prophet of God, in Isaiah 61:1.

When Jesus walked on earth, He had a balanced ministry, meeting the needs of people in three areas: evangelism, healing and deliverance. He fulfilled His "Great Commission" and He instructs us to do the same. "Go ye into all the world and preach—cast out—lay hands on." (Mark 16:15-18)

These were Jesus' last words to His followers. **His last words!**

Does this mean that He was emphasizing something that He wanted carried out? It certainly sounds like that is the case, doesn't it? And we believe that this is our mission as believers of Jesus Christ and children of God.

Many ministries fulfill the need of evangelism, but have very little success in healing and deliverance. Notice that these three needs are found in both "commissions"—that of Jesus and the commission to "them that believe." If Jesus, our example, moved in these three areas, then we must ask ourselves, "Should we move in them, as well?"

JESUS' DELIVERANCE MINISTRY

In searching the scriptures, we have found that a greater part of Jesus' ministry was *deliverance*.

DUMBNESS—look at what the scripture says about dumbness in Matthew 9:32, 33:

(32) As they went out, behold, they brought to him a dumb man possessed with a devil. (33) And when the devil was cast out, the dumb spake: and the multitudes marvelled, saying, It was never so seen in Israel.

There is evidence in the above scripture that this man's dumbness was caused by a *dumb spirit*. How do we know this? Because when the devil was cast out, the previously dumb man could speak!

BLIND AND DUMB—another miracle of Jesus' ministry is seen in Matthew 12:22:

Then was brought unto him one possessed with a devil, blind, and dumb: and he healed him, insomuch that the blind and dumb both spake and saw.

This account shows us that the man had a blind and dumb spirit and when the devil was cast out, he could both see and hear.

UNCLEAN SPIRIT—the scripture describes this spirit in Luke 4:30-35:

(30) But he passing through the midst of them went his way, (31) And came down to Capernaum, a city of Galilee, and taught them

on the sabbath days. (32) And they were astonished at his doctrine: for his word was with power. (33) And in the synagogue there was a man, which had a spirit of an unclean devil, and cried out with a loud voice, (34) Saying, Let us alone; what have we to do with thee, thou Jesus of Nazareth? art thou come to destroy us? I know thee who thou art; the Holy One of God. (35) And Jesus rebuked him, saying, Hold thy peace, and come out of him. And when the devil had thrown him in the midst, he came out of him, and hurt him not.

First, Jesus ministers in **evangelism** (verse 31). And they (the people) were astonished because of His authority (verse 32). Then in verse 34 we see the devil pleading with Jesus to be left alone, acknowledging and fearing His authority. Jesus then moves in **deliverance**, commanding the devil to **hold thy peace and come out of him**. The devil yields to His authority and comes out, after which the man is delivered and not hurt.

FEVER REBUKED—Look at the account of Jesus ministering to Simon Peter's mother-in-law in Luke 4:39:

And he stood over her, and rebuked the fever; and it left her: and immediately she arose and ministered unto them.

Simon Peter's mother-in-law had a fever. Seeing that Jesus rebuked the fever resulting in her immediate recovery is proof that it had to be a living being . . . a spirit.

LEGION—The Word of God tells us in Luke 8:26-33:

(26) And they arrived at the country of the Gadarenes, which is over against Galilee. (27) And when he went forth to land, there met him out of the city a certain man, which had devils long time, and ware no clothes, neither abode in any house, but in the tombs. (28) When he saw Jesus, he cried out, and fell down before him, and with a loud voice said, What have I to do with thee, Jesus, thou Son of God most high? I beseech thee, torment me not. (29) (For he had commanded the unclean spirit to come out of the man. For oftentimes it had caught him: and he was kept bound with chains and in fetters; and he brake the bands, and was driven of the devil into the wilderness.)

(30) And Jesus asked him, saying, What is thy name? And he said,

Legion: because many devils were entered into him. (31) And they besought him that he would not command them to go out into the deep. (32) And there was there an herd of many swine feeding on the mountain: and they besought him that he would suffer them to enter into them. And he suffered them. (33) Then went the devils out of the man, and entered into the swine: and the herd ran violently down a steep place into the lake, and were choked.

The ruling spirit (strong man) resident in this man called himself *Legion*, because there were thousands of them, but regardless of their number, they had to submit. In verse 28 we see that the demons "fell down before him" and actually declared worship to Jesus. Then, becoming aware of his authority, they begged Him not to torment them. When Jesus demanded, "What is thy name?" in verse 30, they responded, "Legion." We see that they yielded to His authority once again. After the man was delivered, we see Jesus' command to him in verse 39:

Return to thine own house, and show how great things God hath done unto thee. And he went his way, and published throughout the whole city how great things Jesus had done unto him.

Now the man could return to his people and live his life as a whole person, TOTALLY SET FREE.

LOOSED FROM INFIRMITY—In Luke 13:11-13, we learn about being *loosed from infirmity:*

And, behold, there was a woman which had a spirit of infirmity eighteen years, and was bowed together, and could in no wise lift up herself. And when Jesus saw her, he called her to him, and said unto her, Woman, thou art loosed from thine infirmity. And he laid his hands on her: and immediately she was made straight, and glorified God.

Satan had bound this woman with a spirit of infirmity for eighteen years. She needed healing but first she had to be loosed, *set free.* Jesus recognized that a spirit was causing her condition and loosed her. Then He laid His hands on her for healing. What a glorious example! Jesus "cast out" and "laid hands on" this woman. As we observe in the previous verse (Luke 13:10) that He was "teaching" in one of the synagogues prior to this event, we can safely conclude that He was moving in all three areas that we mentioned:

evangelism, healing and deliverance.

After reviewing the scriptures, it seems very clear that Jesus not only *believed* in deliverance, He *practiced* it. Jesus came to set the captives free because He believed so strongly in His "Great Commission" that He sought to fulfill it Himself.

What are we going to do with the last words that Jesus gave us? Do we take our "Great Commission" seriously? Do we seek to fulfill it? As His followers, do we follow His example and do what He said to do? Are we really ready to—*go*?

2

To Them That Believe

To Them That Believe

A nd he said unto them, GO YE into all the world, and preach the gospel to every creature. (Mark 16:15)

And these signs shall follow them that believe; In my name shall they cast out devils; they shall speak with new tongues . . . (Mark 16:17)

We need not ponder the last words of Jesus, because we are eager and determined to fulfill the mission God has given to us—our "Great Commission." Jesus, our example, delegated total authority to the believer when He said, "Go ye," and that is what we at this ministry are doing. We are *going*. We believe in evangelism and our first concern when ministering to people is leading them to Christ, if they are not already born again. The Bible says we must get rid of the weight and the sin, and through evangelism, the sin is gone, washed in the blood of Jesus.

Even after salvation, an individual can be burdened down with fear, grief, depression, rejection, addictions, lust, and numerous other bondages. If these weights are not removed, Christians can be so heavy that they become discouraged and want to give up. Deliverance can be of benefit in such circumstances. Through a prayer of deliverance, these weights can be removed and a Christian can then grow and soar in relationship with God.

What is the first sign that Jesus said would follow the believer? *In my name shall they cast out devils. (Mark 16:17)* We, the Body of Christ, have the authority and power to bind and loose every devil in satan's kingdom, and we do it all through Jesus Christ.

And I will give unto thee the keys of the kingdom of heaven: and whatsoever thou shalt bind on earth shall be bound in heaven: and whatsoever thou shalt loose on earth shall be loosed in heaven. (Matthew 16:19)

Our tongue is our weapon and all of heaven backs us when we speak. It is as simple as commanding the spirit to be loosed, then knowing that God promises to confirm His Word with signs following.

Jesus *spoke* with authority because He had the confidence that He *had* supreme authority. The Body of Christ has that same authority through Jesus Christ and it belongs to *every believer*. We inherit the Name of Jesus when we become born again and new creatures in Christ. One of the biggest problems with many Christians is that they believe this God-given authority is for only a "chosen few." This belief results in beaten up, battered, wounded, and defeated Christians who are continually being controlled by evil spirits. These Christians are in bondage and don't even realize it!

We at **Warfare Plus Ministries** share a burden for God's people who are in bondage. We have been called into ministry to help these precious ones get set free, forever. We move in all three areas of ministry to these dear people: evangelism, healing and deliverance— and we know that we are fulfilling our "Great Commission" by doing so. Yes, we know our calling, we have studied the Word of God to gain wisdom and knowledge in this area, and now we are acting on that knowledge. We know our authority and power through Jesus Christ! And we believe that all the children of God can have the same authority and power.

3

Motives

Motives

Things are not always as they appear. You may look good, drive the best car, dress expensively and fashionably, and live in the best neighborhood. You may know the religious "lingo" and pray the most righteous-sounding prayer. But I ask you: Does any of this mean anything to God? NO! As we have heard repeatedly, man looks on the outside, but *God looks on the inside.*

Woe to you, scribes and Pharisees, hypocrites! for ye are like unto whited sepulchres, which indeed appear beautiful outward, but are within full of dead men's bones and of all uncleanness. (Matthew 23:27)

What are your motives?

Why did you marry?

Did you marry your wife because you needed the security of a good-looking woman hanging on your arm, a "trophy" wife?

Did you marry your husband because he was rich and could give you financial security?

Did you marry your spouse because of lust? You should have married for love!

If you married "looks," what will happen if your spouse is severely injured and becomes disfigured or crippled? What will happen when weight is gained, hair falls out, or financial disaster occurs?

Marriage is a commitment for life, for better or for worse.

God is looking at your motives.

Why do you give tithes and offerings?

Have you ever given an offering in order to be recognized? Did you put something in the offering basket so that somebody would see you give and be impressed?

Have you ever offered a large sum of money to a religious project in order to receive recognition? How many times have you been in a church service and the pastor has manipulated the audience while making an appeal for an offering? Did you feel compelled to give against your better judgment?

Do you give an offering in order to receive back for yourself? This is like playing the lottery—and it's happening all over America today!

You should give because the Bible clearly states that we should give a tenth (tithe), and then offer more (offering). Giving should be motivated by love and not manipulation. When you love God and want to please Him, you will want to give and give and give!

So let each one give as he purposes in his heart, not grudgingly or of necessity; for God loves a cheerful giver. (II Cor. 9:7 NKJV)

Why did you get born again?

Did you get born again for selfish reasons? What could be a *selfish* reason for accepting Christ? Well, you could just want to save your skin. If that was your motivation, what is going to happen when you are required to receive a mark on your hand or forehead—or die? Guess what! If your motivation was wrong, you will probably take the mark to save yourself.

God is always searching our hearts and looking at our motives. We need to accept God's pardon from hell because we *love* Him and because He loves us!

Why do you want deliverance?

Is it for selfish reasons? Could it be that devils are tormenting you with nightmares? Maybe they are stealing your love or your finances. Do you want to be set free in order to make life easier for yourself?

We should want to walk free of any demonic influences in our lives because of our love for God. Satan is the archenemy of God (along with his kingdom, of course), and if we truly love God with our whole heart, satan will become our archenemy, too. We will want his influence out of our lives and we will want to destroy him in the lives of our friends, relatives, and mankind, as well.

There is much more to deliverance than just being free. It opens up a channel for God to manifest more of his presence in your life. As He manifests His presence in your life, you begin to walk in His Spirit. As you walk in the Spirit, you will no longer fulfill the "lust of the flesh" in your life.

This I say then, Walk in the Spirit, and ye shall not fulfill the lust of the flesh. (Gal. 5:16)

- Desire God
- Hate the devil
- Crucify the flesh

In order for us to have an intense desire for God, we need to remove all hindrances from our lives; this can be done through the power of deliverance.

God created man because He wanted to have fellowship with him. He is not as interested in your healing ministry, casting out devils, or your success as He is in having a relationship with you. Getting rid of all the demonic influences can help that relationship.

God has an intense desire for you to know Him. One day we will meet Him face to face.

Will you know Him?

Better yet, will He know you?

Well done, good and faithful servant; you have been faithful over a few things, I will make you ruler over many things. Enter into the joy of your lord. (Matt. 25:23 NKJV)

4

Satan's Stronghold Strategy

Satan's Stronghold Strategy

The Spirit of the Lord is upon me, because he hath anointed me to preach the gospel to the poor; he hath sent me to heal the brokenhearted, to preach deliverance to the captives, and recovering of sight to the blind, to set at liberty them that are bruised. (Luke 4:18)

As noted in the first chapter, this scripture was Jesus' *Great Commission*. He went into the synagogue on the Sabbath and read from the book of the prophet Esaias (Isaiah). The Bible tells us He stood up, spoke these words, closed the book, and sat down. This would indicate that Jesus felt like He had said it all, basically wrapping up His entire ministry in one large breath. And here again we see all three elements: evangelism, healing and deliverance.

In His ministry, Jesus fulfilled the prophecy of Isaiah 61:1. This verse talks of those that are bound, and we doubt that few people would disagree with the fact that the bound need to be freed!

Through this scripture we see that deliverance is important, as it is one of the three **needs** mentioned in His Commission, and we know by reading the gospels that He ministered to **needs**.

HE WENT ABOUT SETTING THE CAPTIVES FREE!

So, let's look at this more closely. Why deliverance? The answer can be summed up in one vital, promising word: **freedom**! The next logical question is: **Does a Christian need deliverance?** Those of us in our ministry believe that every born-again Christian should go through deliverance. We do not even pray for deliverance for any-one who is not a Christian (unless they choose to become one before we pray). It is one thing to get free, but it is an entirely different thing to STAY FREE. A person cannot stay free unless he has the power of the Holy Spirit in him, and that power comes only when one is born again.

By now you are probably wondering, "Just exactly what does a

31

Christian need to be free of? Is it possible for a Christian to be possessed? Can a Christian have a demon?" These are the most frequently asked questions when dealing with the subject of deliverance. But we have found that this subject can be very "touchy" for many. Some will consider deliverance but will go no further than the realm of reasoning. Others will frown at the mere mention of the word "deliverance." And unbelief is entertained only because there is no real knowledge or understanding of the subject.

Church, do not let the enemy deceive you any longer!

Don't fall for one of the oldest tricks that satan has up his sleeve: deception! Satan knows if he can stir up confusion and pull you down into doubt, he will defeat you and have the victory. If he can do this, whatever bondage you are in WILL REMAIN. Satan will win and you will LOSE.

Remember the words of God, *My people are **destroyed** for lack of knowledge. (Hosea 4:6)* People of God, rise up against your enemy, the devil! Don't let him destroy you through deception. Reject his lies! Get knowledge and take your stand by refusing to lose the BATTLE!

POSSESSION OR OPPRESSION?

There is a difference between possession and oppression, a huge difference. We know through the Word that we are a trichotomy— spirit, soul and body. *And the Lord God formed man of the dust of the ground* (body), *and breathed into his nostrils the breath of life* (spirit); *and man became a living soul. (Genesis 2:7)*

When we accept Jesus Christ as Lord and Savior, our spirit man is "born again" and we are taught in *II Cor. 5:17: Therefore if any man be in Christ, he is a new creature: old things are passed away; behold, all things are become new.*

If you had a cancer on your arm before you were born again, the cancer would still be there afterward, because the change you experienced was a spiritual change and your body remained the same.

If you had a spirit of fear or rejection before you were born again, you still have that fear and rejection as a Christian, because the experience did not change your soulish man. We have seen *some* people healed and receive partial deliverance during their salvation experience, but this normally does not happen.

Our spirit man becomes a new creature and it is sealed by the Holy Spirit. Satan cannot touch that part of us. Therefore, there can be no **possession.**

Every human being has a God-given gift called a "free will." We all have the right to think or choose whatever we want and no one, not even satan himself, can take that from us. He knows he cannot take total control over us unless we give our will (permission) to him. And for a Christian, that is highly unlikely to happen, because this would mean making a conscious decision to reject Christ and turn your life over to satan, your new master. Satan realizes he cannot take total control, but he tries to get a little stronghold, because a little bit sometimes can go a LONG WAY. And once a stronghold is established, in most cases, he gains more and more ground.

WHAT IS A STRONGHOLD?

Stronghold is a military term meaning a portion of territory that refuses to submit to the ruling authority. Satan wants to establish a little territory of fear, rejection, depression, bitterness, revenge, anger, addiction, lust, perversion, and other bondages in us. These strongholds can begin when we are children through our environment, and also through our inherited bloodline. They start working in our soulish area (emotions, memory, mind and will) and become what we believe is **oppression**. Oppression can become so strong in our lives that it hinders our Christian walk. It can split up marriages, and cause division in churches, businesses, homes and nations.

Many Christians rightfully say they don't have a demon, yet these strongholds are working in their lives. They simply cannot get the victory. These conditions in their lives are certainly not the "fruit of the Spirit" but are, instead, the works of the flesh or situations caused by demonic spirits working. When people continually fall into the same trap over and over and cannot get the **victory**, there is generally oppression present. We know that oppression is not from God, so therefore there must be a demonic force behind every evil work!

Demonic strongholds can hold your spirit man back from being all that God wants you to be. But after they are cast out, you can SOAR with the Lord. **After deliverance, you can mature more in**

33

two weeks than some individuals have in years.

We have counseled with many ministers of the gospel (some are extremely well known) who love God with all their hearts. Yet satan had control over certain areas of their lives, many times in the area of **lust and perversion**! Preachers have told us that sometimes when they are preaching, their eyes will wander across the congregation and fix upon a woman's short skirt. They hate that they are compelled by lust, because it torments them constantly. In fact, most of their time and energy is spent just trying to "cope with the problem."

In almost all of these cases, the ministers had been molested as small children. This molestation gave satan and his kingdom an open door to the spirits of lust and perversion, and resulted in the men becoming very promiscuous in their teen years. After they became born again and received a new spirit man, they still carried all that junk and the memories in their soulish man (mind/emotions/will).

This is where the **battleground** exists because satan has access to and influence in the **soulish part** of a person. Remember, the enemy was there when the event took place in your life and today it is still in your memory. This is the reason people need deliverance: the memory of the problem is still hanging around and terrorizing. **After deliverance, the sting of that memory is gone!**

Before deliverance, satan was playing you like you were a computer. He hit the button labeled "Guilt" and up came a memory of something sinful that you had done.

He pressed the button labeled "Rejection" and up came the memory of a time when you were rejected by someone. And the scenario goes on and on.

After deliverance, you become like a cash register. Satan hits the same old button labeled "Rejection" and to his surprise, a "NO SALE" sign comes up. The devil's trick of torment just does not work anymore. The memory is still there **but the sting is gone**! You are no longer under the enemy's influence.

Salvation. Healing. Deliverance. These have been provided for us and are available to us today. The price has been paid by Jesus Christ on Calvary. At the time of birth, we do not automatically become born again—we have to ask for it, believe it, receive it, then appropriate it! The dictionary defines *appropriate* as "to take exclusive possession of" and that is exactly what we have to do. We must take possession of the gift of God's grace.

When we are born again, we do not automatically become healed; we have to ask for the healing, then believe, receive, and *appropriate* it!

When we are born again, we do not automatically get delivered from all of satan's strongholds. Again, we have to *appropriate* the deliverance!

Deliverance is there for you but you have to want it with your whole heart. You must get to the place where you are so tired of bandaging up the same old wounds that you are willing to take action against the devil and his kingdom, and get completely rid of the wounds.

Every Christian has a tremendous call of God upon his life! Just as Jesus walked on earth and fulfilled His "Great Commission," SO MUST WE! If we are to fulfill this commission effectively, we need to be free of any of satan's baggage. Why be weighted down with his chains any longer? Draw a battle line and declare to satan and his kingdom that he can't cross over it, in Jesus' Name. You can have what the scriptures offer:

(32) And ye shall know the truth, and the truth shall make you free. (36) If the Son therefore shall make you free, ye shall be free indeed. (John 8:32, 36)

FREEDOM IS A GLORIOUS WORD AND IT CAN BELONG TO YOU!

Satan's first step in building a stronghold is a thought. You see, he has a strategy all worked out to get you from Point A to Point B, with a lot of deceitful little steps in between. His goal is to build a stronghold in your life. When satan plants a thought, he is hoping to entrap you in the arena of your reasoning, better known as the **thought realm**. Once you are entangled in his web, you are treading on some very dangerous ground.

The Bible warns us to **bring into captivity every thought** and He teaches us how to do this.

Casting down imaginations, and every high thing that exalteth itself against the knowledge of God, and bringing into captivity every thought to the obedience of Christ. (II Cor. 10:5)

In other words, we are to discern our thoughts. Are they of God? If not, we are to get rid of them! It is a known fact that you cannot keep a thought from coming in, but you can determine how you handle that thought. That's what counts.

When I (Paul) was growing up as a preacher's kid, I was taught that you must watch your actions (the things you say and do).

Abstain from all appearance of evil. (I Thess. 5:22)

I thought, however, that I could think anything I wanted and it wouldn't hurt anybody. If my dad had known some of the thoughts I was having during dinner, he would have choked on his food.

I did not realize that my thoughts were beginning to build strongholds in my life. Satan was putting thoughts in my mind and I was not rejecting them. Frankly, at that time I did not know or understand anything about spiritual warfare and resisting the devil.

Let me emphasize that you cannot keep a thought from entering your mind, but you can choose to reject it. If you entertain evil thoughts, they will develop into imaginations and you will begin toying around with sin in your mind. "What would that be like? How would that sensation feel?" STOP RIGHT THERE! *You are starting to dance*! Right at that moment you need to *cast down those imaginations*. PULL THEM DOWN!

If you allow the imagination to continue to work, it will develop into knowledge and a desire will then be created. This desire will result in a crack in your armor and the seed gets planted. Then satan has something to run with and he is heading into the home stretch. The completion of his strategy will soon be fulfilled in your life. You see, once you have a desire, it is easy for him to push you to the next step: ACTION!

Through satan's influence, you act out what you desire, thus completing his ultimate goal. He has manipulated you from the beginning, from Point A to Point B, and you have not even known it.

RESULT: Now you have a stronghold planted in your life! SATAN HAS YOU IN BONDAGE!

5

Do You Have A Stronghold?

Do You Have A Stronghold?

Submit yourselves therefore to God. Resist the devil, and he will flee from you. (James 4:7)

Many people are puzzled by this scripture and are fully persuaded that it does not work. We are here to tell you, "YES, IT DOES." However, in order for it to work for you, you must properly understand it.

There are three sources of power (or kingdoms):

GOD'S POWER – God has all power, all authority, and is spiritual.

SATAN'S POWER – He has *some* power, but NO authority (he lost it at Calvary) and is spiritual.

SELF POWER – We are physical beings and have no spiritual power, so we must hook up with God or satan in order to gain spiritual power.

Before we were born again, *self* tried to operate in its own power. However, *self* was being influenced by satan's power and, since self-power is physical, it was no match for satan's power.

*In whom **the god of this world** hath blinded the minds of them which believe not, lest the light of the glorious gospel of Christ, who is the image of God, should shine unto them. (II Cor. 4:4)*

Satan is "the god of this world." It is through his influence that strongholds can come into our lives. We can recognize evidence of strongholds when we see a person fall again and again to temptations in a certain area. If you continue to do something that you really don't want to do, you can assume that there is demonic activity present. These strongholds come as a result of our thought life, our heritage, our environment, and sin we have committed in the past.

We believe that satan knew he could not gain the *whole* territory in our lives because of the blood of Jesus, so he decided to settle for just a portion, no matter how small. In order to do this, he had to put his deceitful plan into action and build strongholds in a portion of the territory.

REMEMBER: A stronghold is a portion of territory that refuses to submit to the ruling power.

Examples of some strongholds are:

- **pride, fear, heaviness (grief, depression, rejection)**
- **jealousy (anger, rage, bitterness, revenge)**
- **lying (deceit, profanity)**
- **perversion (lust, pornography)**
- **infirmities (all types of disease known to mankind)**

These are evil spirits and many of the strongholds that have developed prior to our salvation will stay with us even after we receive Jesus as Savior. You see, when we are born again, we hook up to God's power, our spirit man is transformed, and we begin to submit to God. But these strongholds attached themselves to our *soulish man and body* (our emotions, will, memories and senses). As we submit all these areas (strongholds) to God, Jesus Christ becomes not only Savior of our life, but also LORD. *We* are not resisting the devil **but God in us is resisting him**. This is the reason the Bible specifically instructs us to *resist*.

Let's look at the verse in James once again.

Submit yourselves therefore to God. Resist the devil, and he will flee from you. (James 4:7)

We thank God that the scripture is totally right: satan will flee! But we must be submitted to God to gain that authority that makes him go. As children of God, we can *choose* to submit not just *some*, but *all* areas to God. This choice will absolutely demolish any rights that satan has in our lives. Conversely, if you choose NOT to submit, then by your actions you are giving satan permission to stay. THE CHOICE IS YOURS! No one else can make it for you.

SUBMIT OR NOT—**your choice will be the deciding factor as to whether satan stays—or *not*.**

6

Soul Ties - Godly and Ungodly

Soul Ties - Godly and Ungodly

Then he called his twelve disciples together, and gave them power and authority over all devils, and to cure diseases. (Luke 9:1)

O keep my soul, and deliver me: let me not be ashamed; for I put my trust in thee. (Psalm 25:20)

Before we continue with our study of strongholds, let's define and discuss yet another tactic of satan: SOUL TIES. Your soul consists of your **mind, emotions and will**.

We have found that this is one area where people lack knowledge. The most common question we get in our counseling sessions is, "What is a soul tie?"

DEFINITION: Soul tie—when two or more people become bonded together through an emotional situation.

Not all soul ties are evil, however; some can be good—they are either godly or ungodly. Let's explore this a bit further.

GODLY SOUL TIES

Godly soul ties are founded on love. God has ordained and sanctioned these ties between husbands and their wives; parents and their children; friends with friends; Christians with other Christians, as part of the Body of Christ. Let's look at some examples.

HUSBAND AND WIFE
For this cause shall a man leave his father and mother, and shall be joined unto his wife, and they two shall be one flesh. (Eph. 5:31)

It is God's purpose for man and woman to be joined together and become one flesh. Sexual union in marriage is an expression of God's approved love—two become one. That is why there is so much pain, sorrow and trauma in divorce.

Wherefore they are no more twain, but one flesh. What therefore God hath joined together, let not man put asunder. (Matt. 19:6)

PARENT AND CHILD

Jacob had a soul tie with his son, Benjamin.

His life is bound up in the lad's life, and his soul knit with the lad's soul. (Gen 44:30 Amp.)

When parents give love and affection to an infant child, a healthy, godly soul tie is developed. This godly relationship gives love and security to the child and continues throughout his life.

FRIENDS AND FRIENDS

Friends can have a godly soul tie.

The soul of Jonathan was knit with the soul of David, and Jonathan loved him as his own soul. (1 Sam. 18:3 Amp.)

This soul tie between friends was based on pure and holy love.

CHRISTIANS AND CHRISTIANS

Soul ties between Christians are essential so that the Body of Christ can mature and fulfill its great commission. Christians working together in a godly way build strength and unity through the expression of love.

From whom the whole body fitly joined together and compacted by that which every joint supplieth, according to the effectual working in the measure of every part, maketh increase of the body unto the edifying of itself in love. (Eph. 4:16)

UNGODLY SOUL TIES

Ungodly soul ties are generally founded upon lust and develop whenever the spiritual boundaries established by God are violated. A spiritual channel is then established for spirits to flow back and forth. By breaking these ungodly soul ties, you shut down that channel.

MARRIAGE

An ungodly soul tie can develop between a husband and wife if the marriage bed becomes defiled with any perverted act, causing their relationship to become impure. This is sometimes initiated by bringing pornography into the relationship.

FORNICATION AND ADULTERY

What? Know ye not that he which is joined to an harlot is one body? for two, saith he, shall be one flesh. (I Cor. 6:16)

Any sexual relationship outside of marriage establishes ungodly soul ties, and allows lust and perversion to enter in. Petting outside of marriage develops demonic, ungodly emotional soul ties and can open a door for unclean spirits.

Homosexuality and lesbianism form ungodly soul ties between persons of the same sex through perversion and sodomy. God labeled these acts an abomination.

Thou shalt not lie with mankind, as with womankind: it is abomination. (Lev. 18:22)

BESTIALITY

Animals have souls (although they don't have spirits, as people do). Therefore, man can form ungodly soul ties with animals. God calls this "confusion."

Neither shalt thou lie with any beast to defile thyself therewith: neither shall any woman stand before a beast to lie down thereto: it is confusion. (Lev. 18:23)

FAMILY

Ungodly soul ties can also develop within families. A soul tie between a parent and child is godly, healthy and beneficial. However, if there is control and manipulation after the child becomes an adult, it becomes perverted. For instance, when a father gives his daughter in marriage, this signifies a severing of the soul tie, thus allowing a healthy one to be developed between her and her husband. If the parents try to continue the control of their child after marriage, ungodly soul ties develop between the parents and their child and the new spouse. The control and manipulation must stop.

INCEST

Sexual perversion within family relationships has become more and more prevalent. God gives us a warning not to approach anyone who is near of kin to uncover their nakedness (or commit adultery or fornication).

None of you shall approach to any that is near of kin to him, to uncover their nakedness: I am the Lord. (Lev. 18:6)

THE DEAD

And they came to the threshing floor of Atad, which is beyond Jordan, and there they mourned with a great and very sore lamentation: and he made a mourning for his father seven days. (Gen. 50:10)

In Bible times, mourning lasted for only a few days. Mourning is normal and natural, and there is a godly season for mourning the loss of a loved one. However, there is a line that you can cross when you continue mourning beyond what is healthy. The devil will pick up on this and pervert the godly mourning into something ungodly. You open yourself to evil spirits of heaviness, loneliness, grief, self-pity, and depression.

THE BODY OF CHRIST

God wants us to come together and worship Him, and Him alone. The scripture tells us that we are to be joined to God—and God is very jealous.

But he that is joined unto the Lord is one spirit. (I Cor. 6:17)

When man idolizes man, such as a pastor or spiritual leader, rather than Christ, there is an "open door" for satan to work. Spiritual adultery is committed against the Lord when a person comes into idolatry. Every occult practice is a form of idolatry. When you go to a source other than God to receive hidden knowledge, wisdom, guidance and power, you commit spiritual adultery.

CONCLUSION: Godly soul ties are of God—ungodly soul ties are of satan and need to be broken.

ACCOUNT

Through years of experience we have found that spirits refuse to leave a person until their "legal right" to be there has been demolished. We once encountered a young mother who was held in bondage by a spirit of jealousy. This spirit manifested itself intensely and refused to leave. As we ministered to her, the Holy Spirit gave us discernment that we needed to break the ungodly soul ties between her, her ex-husband's present wife, and her half-sister. We led her through what we call "The Proclamation of Forgiveness" and broke the ungodly soul ties. The results were immediate and that spirit of jealousy fled in seconds. Why? Because its legal right to be there was destroyed.

ACCOUNT—Paul's Ungodly Soul Tie

One evening we attended a powerful service at Carpenter's Home Church in Lakeland, Florida, conducted by Rodney Howard-Browne. Driving home after service, we were still in the afterglow of the anointing of the Holy Spirit, when I heard a voice in my spirit say, "You need to break the ungodly soul ties between you and your father." I quickly thought to myself, "That's not necessary." My father was a godly man, a minister of the gospel for over forty years, and we had a healthy relationship. A few moments passed and then the same voice said, "If you break the ungodly soul ties between you and your father, I will heal your sinus problem right now."

All my life I had fought a severe sinus problem that caused an irritating drainage in the back of my throat. I was on antibiotics or antihistamines almost constantly. I had asked God to heal me and had been prayed for many times, but nothing ever happened.

My father had the same battle; his sinuses were so bad that he always preached with a microphone in one hand and a handkerchief in the other. His father (my grandfather) had died at a relatively early age from pneumonia. We have learned that spirits of infirmity also can be familiar spirits that come from generational curses.

As we drove down the freeway, I shared with Claire what God had just said to me, and she immediately reached into her purse and brought out the anointing oil. When God says NOW, there is not a second to waste. We began to pray and before I knew what was happening, Claire anointed me with oil. I felt an urgency to really get down to business in prayer, so I raised my voice and spoke these words with authority, "I break the ungodly soul tie between me and my father and his ancestors, and between my father and me." Then I put what we call a "Jesus bloodline" between my father and me and continued praying with God-given authority and power. **"Satan, you and your kingdom cannot cross this Jesus bloodline. Spirit of infirmity and sinus trouble, I command you to leave me NOW in the Name of Jesus."**

Suddenly I felt something leave through my fingertips, as well as through the top of my head. Within forty-five seconds, my lifelong battle was finally over—my sinuses completely dried up and have

47

remained healthy ever since.

There was a generational curse that had to be broken before I could receive my healing. The spirit of infirmity had to leave after the ungodly soul tie was broken and the spirit was commanded to leave. It had to leave—it had no choice but to go. You see, it had lost its legal right to be there! Thank God for the blood of the Lamb and the fact that He took the curse for us at Calvary!

Before we close this chapter, let's take a look at a few additional accounts of deliverance. These will clearly demonstrate the importance of breaking ungodly soul ties. Sometimes we are *amazed* to see how ungodly soul ties can hold so many people in bondage and ultimately destroy countless lives.

ACCOUNT

Recently a well-known woman named Vivian came to us for deliverance. After several weeks of counseling, instruction, and preparation, we felt it was time to proceed with her deliverance.

During the deliverance session, we discerned that there was an ungodly soul tie between her and a girlfriend who had committed suicide three years earlier. While we were in the process of breaking this ungodly soul tie, the demon in her began screaming and thrashing her body about. It was obvious that this demon was furious and wanted to fight. We were thankful that the battle was short and the ungodly soul tie was broken. Afterwards, we commanded a spirit of suicide to leave her, as well, and again, this spirit created a tremendous commotion and resistance before leaving.

Next, we called out a spirit of death, and as soon as we called it forth, we witnessed something we had never seen before. Vivian's hands instantly changed colors, turning yellow, beginning at her fingertips and going up to her elbows. It looked like she suddenly had developed jaundice.

After the deliverance session, we mentioned her hands to her, because we had all noticed the manifestation. She told us this had happened to her before, when her husband was dying. While he lay dying, he had grasped her hands tightly and would not let go. As soon as her husband expired, Vivian looked at her hands and noticed that they had become yellow. We knew right away that a spirit of death had transferred to her when her husband died.

The yellow appearance changed back to normal immediately after we came against that spirit of death and cast it out. When the color changed back to normal, it started at her elbows and went right out her fingertips—the reverse of how it entered. And it left much faster than it had come. Whoosh! It was gone!

NOTE: **There was an ungodly soul tie between Vivian and her friend, and also her husband, that allowed the spirit of death to enter.**

ACCOUNT—Molested in Diapers

We always break ungodly soul ties before we pray for a person's deliverance. Marilyn was a beautiful woman in her early thirties, a very gifted actress who had played a major role in a television series for ten years. She had played numerous roles in other productions over the years, and multi-personality spirits had attached themselves to her. We found that the multi-personality spirits would NOT leave until we broke the ungodly soul ties between her and the names of the characters that she had played.

When we began the deliverance, she mentioned that she had always had an uneasy feeling about her boy cousins, so we immediately broke anything that could be ungodly between them. She went on to tell us that when these cousins came to her house, she always went into her bedroom and stayed until they left. During the deliverance session, she screamed so loudly and so intensely that her face became blotchy and she screamed out, "It's my first birthday! I am still in my diapers! My cousins are holding me down—I can feel their hands on my wrists! They are sexually molesting me!"

She became so *intense* that *black patches* appeared under her eyes and she looked like she had been in a fistfight. We stopped her and had her do a proclamation "to choose to forgive her boy cousins." After that, we commanded those spirits to leave and they obeyed *immediately*.

Even though she had no memory of the incident until the time of deliverance, she had put a shield around herself and never let a relationship with a man come into her life. She was extremely beautiful, but she had never had a boyfriend. After we prayed, she accepted a date with a man that same week, and she told us later that she really enjoyed his company. "I told him that if he had asked me out a week earlier, I would not have accepted," she said. Now she is free to live a normal life and relate to the opposite sex without fear.

ACCOUNT—Carrie

Carrie had been waiting patiently for almost two years to get an appointment with us. When we were finally able to see her, she was so excited about the deliverance that she could hardly wait to do the homework we had given her! She had even fasted prior to the appointment.

As we gathered information about ungodly soul ties, right in the middle of it, the Lord told me, "FIRE!" The Lord spoke this word to me three times before I finally asked her, "Carrie, what about a fire?" Carrie was speechless for a moment, startled!

It seems that when she was about five years old, her little friend from next door had caught fire, right in front of her. Carrie had watched her friend burn. Later, in a tragic accident, Carrie was lighting a fire in a fireplace and the house suddenly ignited. The house burned quickly and there was nothing left but ashes.

The ungodly soul tie that needed to be broken was between her and her friend who had died. This had given an entry point for a spirit of fear to come into her life.

Although Carrie was born again and Spirit-filled, she could not live victoriously and be all that God wanted her to be because this fear was always holding her back. For her, life was like hitting a brick wall head-on. You cannot have perfect faith if you are plagued with a spirit of fear. Now that the spirit of fear is gone, she is experiencing perfect faith.

There is no fear in love; but perfect love casteth out fear: because fear hath torment. He that feareth is not made perfect in love. (I John 4:18)

Over the years, the Lord has given us insight into many of these ungodly soul ties that need to be broken.

CONCLUSION: Before we pray deliverance for a person, there are certain steps and procedures that must be taken. Each one serves a unique purpose to ensure a complete and successful deliverance. After the individual receives counseling and completes the homework assignments, we break all ungodly soul ties. Then we can proceed to the strongholds—so let's go on to Chapter Seven and the stronghold forces!

7

Stronghold Forces

Stronghold Forces

*B*ut *let him ask in faith, nothing wavering. For he that wavereth is like a wave of the sea driven with the wind and tossed. (James 1:6)*

The Lord looked down from heaven upon the children of men, to see if there were any that did understand, and seek God. (Psalm 14:2)

In this chapter you will see examples of strongholds, along with brief explanations, to give you an idea of what you may or may not be dealing with. We share true accounts of deliverance from these strongholds. We have found that praying for a person's deliverance in this particular order works and as we describe each one, the explanation will be revealed. Deliverance is a call to holiness. Before we pray for someone, we have him/her close all the doors of the past.

Let us examine these strongholds more closely.

HAUGHTY
Pride goeth before destruction and an haughty spirit before a fall. (Prov. 16:18)

- Pride   Prov. 6:16, 17
- Perfection
- Accusation
- Competition
- Mockery
- Stubbornness
- Self-righteousness   Luke 18:11,12
- Gossip   Prov. 23:23, 24
- Self-exaltation   I Peter 5:5
- Judgmental
- Selfish
- Condemning

We always pray for this spirit first because pride and stubbornness will hinder a person's ability to receive deliverance. When you get rid of these spirits first, the person does not care how they act or what takes place during the deliverance.

Demons of haughtiness invite in the demons that you see listed in that category. They are a little "clique" and usually manifest themselves in similar ways. They manifest themselves by causing the person to sit up very erect while giving others a look as if to say "You're a low life." They feel they are superior to others and have a tendency to laugh a lot (sometimes with a sound best described as a *cackle*).

We notice that these spirits will group together—one will open the door for another.

ACCOUNT

We commanded a spirit of pride to go from a lady in a group session and the spirit spoke up, "She likes me, she likes me, she likes me!" The lady spoke this as she sat very erect, looking down her nose at us. Then she began to make a cackling sound. We reminded the spirit that it had no legal right in this woman's body and then we commanded it to go, in the Name of Jesus. It left immediately and the woman was free!

ACCOUNT—Claire

Recently we were conducting a seminar when we had a face-to-face confrontation with the most powerful spirit of pride and haughtiness we had ever encountered. Jolene was a very prim and proper woman in her thirties. She wore her curly blond hair piled high on her head and had a very cold demeanor. Although she did not raise her hand when we asked about praying for those who had pride, it was obvious to us that she had a real problem.

I passed by her chair and casually asked her if I could pray for her. She straightened up in her chair and very haughtily told me that it would be all right if I really thought she needed it.

Paul sat down in front of her and began to call out a spirit of haughtiness/pride. Immediately a manly voice came out of her and said with a pronounced British accent, "I am from England and I am *not* coming out. There are 9,000 of us and we are not about to leave."

Where did that come from? We found that her ancestors came from England and the spirits came directly down through her inherited bloodline. We had to spend time breaking ungodly soul ties between Jolene, her parents, and their ancestors.

We discovered that Jolene had spent many years in a mental institution because whenever these spirits in her manifested, people thought she was insane.

We once prayed deliverance for a person in a mental institution and within two hours' time, he was as normal as a person can possibly be. Many people have come to us who have been diagnosed as mentally ill, and in our prayer for them the only problem we have seen was a demon manifesting. Sometimes I wonder how many dear people are trapped in mental hospitals by satan when all they really need is deliverance in mind and body.

I pray that more Christians will hear the battle call and help set people free.

DEAF AND DUMB
And one of the multitude answered and said, "Master, I have brought unto thee my son, which has a dumb spirit"…When Jesus saw that the people came running together, he rebuked the foul spirit, saying unto him, Thou dumb and deaf spirit, I charge thee, come out of him, and enter no more into him. (Mark 9:17, 25)

- Mental Illness   Matt. 17:15
- Insanity   Mark 9:17-29
- Seizures/Epilepsy   Mark 9:10, 16,18
- Double Mindedness
- Suicidal   Mark 9:22
- Multi-personality
- Hyperactivity
- Self-mutilation   Mark 5:5

Jesus cast out the spirit from the boy who had seizures (Mark 9:25), calling it a deaf and dumb spirit (because it was the *ruling* spirit).

At least fifty percent of the people we pray for have a spirit of mental illness and insanity. Most of the time, the spirit is just lying dormant, having never manifested; it has come down through the inherited bloodline.

It is extremely important to call multi-personality spirits by name. If you speak in general terms and say, "I command any spirits that are not the born-again Ann (or John or Sue) to come out," usually nothing happens; the spirit will not respond. It may show up and manifest, but many times it will not come out until you call it by name. The following story illustrates this point.

> A teacher returns to her classroom and observes children in the back row acting up and making lots of noise. "All of you who are making noise, come to the front," she says loudly. Not surprisingly, nothing happens. The children just look at each other, shrug, and say, almost in unison, "It wasn't me."
>
> However, if she enters the classroom and says with authority, "Johnny, come to the front immediately," she will get results. Johnny will come to the front of the room for two reasons: first, he obeys the *authority* of the teacher and, second, she has *identified* him *personally*.

This is the procedure we use in deliverance, especially when we call out multi-personalities. We begin by asking the person if she/he has ever felt like someone else. If so, does that "other" have a name? Sometimes you can detect what kind of spirit it is by the way the spirit manifests or sometimes you can simply say, "You spirit that is manifesting, I command you to come out in Jesus' Name."

Many times the multi-personality spirit will speak through the person and use a different voice (for example, a woman may speak with a man's voice and vice versa). Sometimes the multi-personality comes in during a time of the person's life when he/she is using a nickname. If so, try to identify the multi-personality by calling it by the *nickname*. The deliverance is much more successful after you identify the name of the multi-personality. Often the multi-personality will look at you with an extremely shocked expression, as if to ask, "How did you ever find me?" They actually like to hide from the person until they are ready to do their takeover. Many times the person doesn't even know that they have a multi-personality spirit.

If a person was rejected a great deal as a little child, and this continues through his life, there is generally a personality of rejection, as well as a spirit of rejection.

We recently prayed for a man who had indulged in so much perversion that a spirit of perversion manifested itself as a separate multi-personality. Once we called out the personality of perversion, everything broke and his deliverance was very smooth. You see, the eventual deliverance came easily because the major spirit had left him.

ACCOUNT—Multi-personalities

We had never experienced as many different faces in one human being as Heather possessed. She was plagued with multi-personalities and when each one surfaced, it became totally believable and real. Each personality had its own distinctive facial expression and body language and as each new personality surfaced, it was difficult for us to believe that this was the same girl who had come to us begging for an appointment.

Heather's husband was in prison for sexually abusing their son, Ronnie. Ronnie had been removed from his mother's care and this left her in a serious suicidal state. She longed to be free! Her true "born-again" personality desperately wanted freedom and longed for deliverance. The other personalities were clearly terrified, but this did not stop the evil personalities from doing physical battle to keep their territory.

This deliverance session was very interesting and quite long. The personality that made Heather sad and depressed distorted her facial features and she looked like she was being tortured horribly. We encountered a personality of vanity and pride that would stand up and actually mock us and laugh, sneering as she looked down her nose at us.

When we discerned a personality of lust, perversion and whoredom and called out these spirits, they began to act extremely sensuous.

That personality caused Heather to lick her lips slowly and make very seductive body movements. Her hair fell across her face and her eyes begged Paul for his attention. The demon obviously was trying to beguile him, perhaps because that devil thought it could persuade Paul not to command it to go. But he rose up mightily, and with all power and authority in the Name of Jesus, he commanded the multi-personality spirit to leave. Heather told us that this spirit, whom she called "Cassandra," would come over her at night, causing her to do evil things she ordinarily would never do.

We really had a battle with these multi-personalities, but the victory was oh, so sweet! Heather doesn't have to fight them anymore. She no longer cries for freedom, because Jesus made her free forever— she is a wonderful, beautiful person that people love to be around.

SLUMBER

Yet a little sleep, a little slumber, a little folding of the hands to sleep: So shall thy poverty come as one that travelleth, and thy want as an armed man. (Prov. 6:10, 11)

- Withdrawal
- Mind binding
- Sleepiness
- Forgetfulness
- Stupidity
- Daydreaming
- Trances
- Confusion
- Inactivity
- Lethargy
- Sluggishness

ACCOUNT—Claire

These spirits sometimes make you feel like your head is full of mud. The spirit of stupidity binds up a child's mind and keeps him from learning in school. I had a spirit of sleepiness and when Paul prayed for me, I got sleepier than I had ever been in my entire life. My head dropped to the side and I just wanted to sleep.

Paul kept screaming at me and, frankly, all I could think of was punching him in the nose. "I wish he would just shut up so I can sleep!" I felt like I could sleep for two weeks straight. Then I heard him say, "In the Name of Jesus, I command you to open your eyes!" I opened my eyes and I felt that spirit lift and leave. It left with a big yawn and I was instantly wide awake and more alert than ever.

ACCOUNT—Claire

When we first began our deliverance ministry, we were praying for a friend, calling out a spirit of slumber. But I discerned a "mind binding" spirit, a spirit of confusion, and as I called it out, this friend's eyes took on a blank stare. Then his eyes filled with tears and he suddenly jumped and I could tell the mind binding spirit had left him. Later we were discussing his deliverance and he said, "I felt something leave me that was really cold; it left out the top and both sides of my head."

We saw him a few months later and he commented, "Prior to my deliverance session, I would be in service listening to the pastor read the scripture, paying close attention. Then he would ask if we all understood the scripture and people would agree that they did. But I would keep thinking to myself, 'Am I the only dummy in the place? What's wrong with me?' Because I would have to read a scripture a dozen times or more before I would really understand it."

He went on to tell us that after the spirit left him, he could read and understand the scriptures and the words would even jump off the page at him. "I am so blessed because that spirit of mind binding is gone. Now I have clarity where before there was so much confusion." He was so joyful!

FAMILIAR
Then said Saul unto his servants, Seek me a woman that hath a familiar spirit, that I may go to her, and inquire of her. And his servants said to him, Behold, there is a woman that hath a familiar spirit at Endor. (I Sam. 28:7)

And when they shall say unto you, Seek unto them that have familiar spirits, and unto wizards that peep, and that mutter: should not a people seek unto their God? for the living to the dead? (Is. 8:19)

- Necromancer   Deut. 18:11
- Clairvoyant   I Sam. 28:7, 8
- Spirit Guides
- Inherited Curses
- **Curses**:
    Witch or Warlock
    Indian Curses
    Santeria Curses
    Roots Curses
    Voodoo Curses
    Words that have been spoken
- Occult
- Astrology
- Horoscope
- Fortune telling
- Seances

Familiar spirits are very strong. When people get involved in satanism and occult activity, they are dealing with a higher level of devils. The Lord is not intimidated at all—this is a piece of cake for Him. Most of us have familiar spirits from our bloodlines. The devils like to stay in the same family because they are "familiar" with it. They know exactly which family member they can get to make you angry, or to make you feel rejected, or to put a guilt trip on you. The only people the devil can use to "get to" you are those who are very close to you (because you do not care what strangers say or think).

These familiar spirits like to stay in your bloodline because people die but spirits do not. Therefore, when a family member dies, any evil spirit they had will go immediately to another family member who will allow the spirit to enter.

Thou shalt not bow down thyself to them, nor serve them: for I the Lord thy God am a jealous God, visiting the iniquity of the fathers upon the children unto the third and fourth generation of them that hate me. (Ex. 20:5)

It is extremely important to break ungodly soul ties between the individual and the parents and ancestral line. It is also important to break soul ties with anyone they may have been involved with in the occult world.

Demons are just waiting for humans to call on them. For example, just start using a Ouija board and they show up. The same thing happens with palm readers, seances, eastern meditation or any other occult activity. But the other side of the coin is glorious—there are a host of God's mighty angels just waiting for you to call on them. **And the good news is that there are twice as many angels on God's side as there are on satan's side**.

Many times familiar spirits leave through the same spots where they came in. For example, a woman who came for deliverance had been cut in many parts of her body during an occult ritual years before. When the demons were called out, they left her through the same spots where she had been cut. Every time a demon left, she would cry out in pain and grab various parts of he body, such as her shoulder or her thigh. We knew these points of exit were also the places of entrance.

As part of our preliminary teaching of those who come to us for deliverance, we have individuals write down all occult activities in which they have been involved. Then we have them read a proclamation out loud (because the demons cannot read their mind) to renounce them! Next, we have them break any ungodly soul ties with anyone in the occult world, especially any group leader or person who has hypnotized them, or any spirit guides that entered through meditation or martial arts.

After they write down the names of people and things from their occult past and speak their proclamation of renouncing, we have them burn the paper. On many occasions, we have had people try to burn the paper only to find out that the paper would not burn! One person told us that a sulfur odor came out of the paper and another told us that he heard screams when he tried to burn his paper.

One lady told us that after unsuccessfully trying to burn her list three times, she soaked it with lighter fluid and it still would not burn. Finally, she said, "I command you in the Name of Jesus to burn!" To her utter astonishment, the paper practically blew up in her face!

The main reason we have people burn their list is because they are now doing something in the physical that they have just done in the spiritual realm. They have "burned the bridge" that allowed satan into their lives through the occult, and have closed the door forever. Now they are ready for complete deliverance by kicking the demons out of their lives. Deliverance is just that: kicking the devil out of your life! Preparing and burning the list is not the actual deliverance, but this action closes the door to any legal right the demonic kingdom has to be in or around you. Deliverance from all occult demons is a snap.All it takes is a command from a born-again believer who knows his authority in Jesus!

We have learned that almost all occult groups use the Bible to some degree. They may use the Name of Jesus or God, or even the Holy Spirit. Also, they usually do some good things in their community as a sort of cover-up. Many have statues of Mary and Jesus standing in the midst of their demonic objects and some may gather together and disguise themselves as churches. If you are not a born-again believer, and do not know what the Bible teaches, you are a prime candidate for being sucked in to their clutches.

Many occult groups have their members working full-time on college campuses, recruiting for their groups. We recently counseled an individual in the occult who had been assigned to the University of South Florida. We have also discovered that many witches' covens have members who are assigned to a church. They go to churches, behave like regular members, speak the right language, pray the right prayers, and look just like everyone else in the congregation. There may be some in your church; you could be sitting beside a witch next Sunday and not even know it. They are assigned to good Christian, Bible-believing churches that are making a difference in the spirit realm, where people are hearing about salvation and getting born again.

Demons come with pretty faces and are assigned to a church to divide the congregation and destroy the ministry. Their goal is to ruin a pastor or cause a church split. We have counseled many, many ex-witches and occult people, and you would never guess by looking at them that they have been so destructive and evil. We wish that Christians were as devoted to the cause of spreading the gospel as witches are to tearing it down.

ACCOUNT

Once a month we hold a four-day seminar for anyone who wants to attend. During this seminar we conduct a group deliverance session with everyone present.

Recently, Paul took our car to be repaired and Ken, the shop owner, asked Paul what he did for a living. When Ken (a Catholic) found out we were in deliverance ministry, he went wild with emotion. "I was just praying that the Lord would lead me to someone who knows and understands deliverance!" Later, he attended a session and was so impressed by what he saw that he went back to his church and told everyone about the sessions. There was such a drastic change in his life that several men he knew realized they needed deliverance, as well.

Ken had purchased a large supply of our teaching materials and spent all his free time taking the men through the counseling teaching and the related homework. Then he called and asked if we would hold a deliverance session just for them. He not only brought them to the session, but he even helped out in the deliverance itself.

Henry, one of the men Ken brought, began to manifest tremendously when Paul called out a familiar spirit from his inherited bloodline. Henry immediately stiffened up and his hands became twisted and deformed. Paul asked him if anyone in his family had arthritis or palsy and he answered that his mother was plagued with arthritis and his father had palsy. Those spirits had attached themselves to Henry and even though they were dormant, they were just waiting for the right time to manifest. The other two friends who had come with Ken were astonished at what they saw happening and as their friend continued to manifest demons, they almost lost it!

Paul commanded the familiar spirits to leave in Jesus' Name, and as he spoke, Henry's body went from being totally rigid to completely limp as each spirit left. Then Paul came against the spirit of infirmity, and as the spirit fled, Henry's left ear opened up and he could hear. He had been completely deaf in that ear! He also received healing in his elbow from constant pain that he had been living with for ten years.

After the session, Henry picked up the chair and looked under it. When Paul asked if he had lost something, Henry replied, "I thought that you had the chair wired because it felt like 220 volts of electricity went through my body. I'm still numb from the waist down."

These men were set free by the power of God and it certainly caused a stir in their church. Our phone is still ringing with others wanting to attend our seminars.

DIVINATION

And it came to pass, as we went to prayer, a certain damsel possessed with a spirit of divination met us, which brought her masters much gain by soothsaying: The same followed Paul and us, and cried, saying, These men are the servants of the most high God, which shew unto us the way of salvation. (Acts 16:16-18)

- Soothsayer   Micah 5:12
- Fortune telling
- Horoscope
- Stargazer-Zodiac   Is. 47:13
- Occult
- Witch/warlock   Ex. 22:18
- Magic (white/black)   Ex. 7:11 and 8:7
- Seances

FEAR

For God hath not given us the spirit of fear, but of power, and of love, and of a sound mind. (II Tim. 1:7)

- Insecurity
- Inadequacy
- Inferiority Complex
- Timidity
- Worry
- Sensitivity
- Fear of Authority
- Terror (sense of danger)
- Torment/Horror   Ps. 55:5
- Nightmares   Ps. 91:5, 6
- Phobias (dark, heights, future)
- Anxiety
- Nervous
- Insomnia
- Abandonment
- Panic attacks

The spirits of fear are deadly and can kill. They usually manifest by having a person shake, holding his body as if it is freezing cold, his face contorted with terror. We believe that this stronghold destroys more Christians than any other and it holds God's people back from accomplishing their assignments. Our experience shows us that ninety percent of the people we pray for have some form of FEAR. When we pray against a spirit of fear and it leaves, that person's faith increases and a great boldness takes hold.

ACCOUNT

We have found through painful experience that it is extremely important to break the power of any medication in a person's body before we begin to pray deliverance. A couple of times we have forgotten to do so, and we have had some unfortunate experiences, because it can hinder the entire deliverance process.

Denise, a brand-new Christian, had been in a mental institution several times. On more than one occasion she had tried to commit suicide (the last time only a couple of weeks before we saw her). She was a surprisingly likable person, very loving and sincere, but a spirit of heaviness was obvious in her personality. She seemed so sad and unhappy.

As we prayed, it seemed that nothing was happening, but when we spoke to the spirit of fear, she began to shake uncontrollably. Even her teeth were chattering! It is impossible to make one's body shake like hers was shaking, and she was pitiful to watch. Poor little thing! She was so frightened, because IT was in control, not Denise. She could not stop the shaking and her eyes pleaded with us to stop the process.

We commanded the spirit to stop manifesting and to leave, but it would not cooperate. The thought of medication ran through my head. We immediately started to break the power of any medication in her body and commanded that it not hinder her deliverance. We even broke the power of the medications one by one by the name of the drug. Once this was done, the demons left immediately, and she was miraculously set free! If you take any kind of medication, we recommend that you pray over it before taking it, asking God to cause it to help you, not harm you.

ACCOUNT

In the beginning of our ministry, we prayed for Beth, a woman who had made her own home a prison. She was so afraid of someone coming into her home that she kept the doors and windows locked at all times, and wouldn't even leave the house by herself. On the Sunday morning she came to us, her voice and hands were shaking as she asked us to pray for deliverance from the fear. We scheduled her for an appointment.

We had two counseling sessions with Beth before her deliverance session. When we called out a spirit of phobic fear of being around people, her body shook uncontrollably. The shaking was so severe that we thought her would skin would fly off her body.

Suddenly, that spirit of phobic fear left her and all was calm. She now takes walks around the block, drives her car, and is active in her church. She is a real woman of God and God did a great work in her life by setting her free.

HEAVINESS
To appoint unto them that mourn in Zion, to give unto them beauty for ashes, the oil of joy for mourning, the garment of praise for the spirit of heaviness; that they might be called trees of righteousness, the planting of the Lord, that he might be glorified. (Is. 61:3)

- Rejection
- Despair
- Grief
- Fatigue
- Guilt
- Self-pity   Ps. 69:20
- Loneliness
- Depression
- Manic Depression
- Gloominess and Sadness
- Insomnia

Heaviness always manifests in the same way: the spirit comes in with tears and leaves with tears. Rejection usually comes in when one is a small child. The devil then sets that person up for the rest of his life to feel rejection from those close to him. The devil feeds, waters and cultivates that seed of rejection.

When a person realizes that the devil is just using other people to feed that seed of rejection he has planted (rather than actually being rejected), anger at the devil sets in. The devil gets exposed and then he gets expelled!

Many times a parent will favor one child over another and this opens the door for the spirit of rejection to enter the child that is not favored. Many times the favorite child will get a spirit of guilt. Another way the spirit of guilt enters is when someone has been a party to abortion. Therefore, it is necessary for an ungodly soul tie to be broken between the unborn child and that person, and also between the sexual partner that brought about the pregnancy. If this ungodly soul tie is not broken, the spirit of guilt will not leave; satan and his kingdom are legalists and if he has a legal right to stay, he will!

ACCOUNT

A pastor's wife came to us with a lot of fear and asked if we would pray for her for deliverance. A year or so earlier, her brother, with whom she was very close, passed away, and she was consumed with grief. Whenever she heard a specific song on the radio, she burst into tears, or when she looked at his picture, she broke down and cried. This spirit of grief had been so powerful in her life that she had become very depressed, resisted going anywhere, and rarely left her home She just wanted to stay home, alone, depressed.

The Bible says that when a loved one dies, we are to grieve for a time, but we are not to allow grief to linger. However, this lady had let grief linger and she was not letting go. This opened a door in her life that allowed a spirit of grief to enter. Even though her relationship with her brother had been wholesome, an ungodly soul tie had developed after his death because she wouldn't let go of the grief. We broke that soul tie and put a Jesus bloodline between her and her deceased brother. A tremendous manifestation took place when the soul tie broke; then we were able to call out the spirit of grief and she was set free!

After her deliverance, she became very free and extroverted and was even able to sing a solo before a large crowd, something she was never able to do before her deliverance. God did a mighty work in her life!

REJECTION

Rejection is dominated by two larger strongholds: **fear and heaviness**. Although rejection is not the ruling spirit, we have concluded that it is a parental spirit. By this we mean that it breeds other spirits and destroys many lives.

When a child is unwanted, a door opens for rejection. For instance, the parents may not be financially ready for the child, the parents may be going through a divorce, or the child may be born out of wedlock. Also, rejection can be felt when favoritism by the parents is shown.

This seed is usually planted when a child is very small, sometimes even in the mother's womb. Then it germinates and satan's kingdom begins to feed the spirit by continually working through other people, putting more and more rejection upon the unsuspecting victim. Soon the child may find that neighborhood children do not want to play with him or, later, kids at school may not allow him to be in their "clique." During his teen years, his girlfriend may leave him, then in his thirties his wife may leave him for another man.

These are hypothetical examples, of course, yet they all feed the spirit of rejection. The rejection becomes so deeply rooted that by the time a person reaches his middle thirties, he finds it extremely difficult to cope. It is just one big set-up from the beginning, starting with the planting of the seed.

As we mentioned before, we have noticed that rejection will breed other spirits in people's lives. It seems to branch two ways:

1. It opens the door for despair, grief, self-pity, loneliness, depression and then *suicide*.
2. It opens the door for bitterness, revenge, anger, hatred, rage, wrath, then *murder*.

No matter which branch it may take, the end result is always the same: DEATH. This kind of demonic activity brings light to the fact that satan and his kingdom have come to steal, kill and destroy.

Jesus came to give you life and give it more abundantly. If you can have abundant life, why settle for anything less? BREAK THE POWER

OF REJECTION in your life and enjoy what the Lord has for you!

ACCOUNT—Double Blessing

Margaret had a mighty deliverance; in fact, she received deliverance the same day she received salvation. Her father committed suicide when she was only five years old and satan convinced her that she was to blame for her father's suicide. She experienced mental and sexual abuse from family members and baby-sitters, and her life was filled with rejection. Satan's kingdom had set her up from childhood with spirits of rejection and guilt.

Margaret was in her late teens when she accepted Jesus Christ as her personal Savior. The person who led her to the Lord understood deliverance and prayed for her deliverance only minutes after she was born again. A double blessing! She states that she knew beyond a shadow of doubt that demons were present and she knew when they left her because she felt a tremendous release. This lady teaches the Word of God all over the world with signs following and God is using her mightily.

This is a perfect example of what the Lord can do with people when nothing is hindering them, when there is NOTHING TO HOLD THEM IN BONDAGE! They are free to fulfill their *great commission* and live life victoriously.

How much more abundant can life be?

JEALOUSY

And the Lord spake unto Moses, saying, Speak unto the children of Israel, and say unto them, If any man's wife go aside, and commit a trespass against him, And a man lie with her carnally, and it be hid from the eyes of her husband, and be kept close, and she be defiled, and there be no witness against her, neither she be taken with the manner; And the spirit of jealousy come upon him, and he be jealous of his wife, and she be defiled: or if the spirit of jealousy come upon him, and he be jealous of his wife, and she be not defiled...(Numbers 5:11-14)

- Impatience
- Bitterness
- Strife
- Covetousness
- Control (Jezebel)
- Revenge   Prov. 14:16
- Retaliation
- Suspicion
- Anger   Prov. 22:24
- Rage   Prov. 6:34
- Hatred   Gen. 37:4
- Wrath
- Murder   Gen. 4:8
- Violence
- Restlessness
- Selfishness

These spirits will manifest with strength far beyond what is humanly possible. In one instance, we had to have several people restrain a small, 110-pound woman. When praying deliverance, you will always need two people or more to help you, and at least one of them should be male. Spirits in the jealousy category will want to fight, and being opposed physically seems to empower them. When we take our hands off a person, the demon will usually calm down.

The person being dealt with for jealousy must forgive everyone who has hurt him in the past. Some event occurred in the past that allowed the spirit to enter, so if the spirit does not leave immediately after the prayer of deliverance, ask the person who in his life needs his forgiveness. Then have the individual speak a proclamation out loud to forgive the person(s).

ACCOUNT

The telephone rang and the man on the other end of the line told me that we had prayed deliverance for his son and he wanted the prayer of deliverance also. There were things in his life that scared him.

The next week this man came into our group sessions to be prayed for. As we prayed and called out a spirit of jealousy, there was a tremendous manifestation of strength. He was small, weighing only about 130 pounds, but he was a karate champion and that evening he exhibited the strength of at least ten big men. We thank God we had some strong men present in the session when he took his karate stance.

Spirits of revenge and retaliation manifested but as we came against them and commanded them to leave in the Name of Jesus, the man was completely set free! When he was free from the bondage, the room became so holy that he fell to his knees and raised his hands toward heaven. As he praised God, it felt like the windows of heaven opened. The glory of the Lord filled the room and there was an awesome manifestation of the Holy Spirit. It was glorious!

We have often observed this presence of the Lord after we have prayed deliverance for people. It is so remarkable and beautiful, and everyone is incredibly blessed by His presence.

This man later told a testimony of becoming so uncontrollable that he was afraid he would hurt his family. After his deliverance he began a victorious life, freed by the power of Jesus.

ACCOUNT—Paul

Sammy had lived in a third world country as a child and had moved to the Tampa Bay area as a teenager. In his native country he had observed his parents' activities in Santeria, an occult religion which combines West African and Roman Catholic beliefs. This opened many doors for occult activity in his life. After Sammy moved to Tampa, he accepted Jesus Christ as Lord and Savior, but he was in bondage to something that made him behave irrationally and violently.

Sammy married a wonderful young woman and they had three lovely children, but he often had a spirit of suspicion overcome him. He was so suspicious of his wife that he would call her almost every hour of the day to check on her. He accused her of having affairs and doing other things behind his back, even though she was a faithful, born-again Christian woman. This spirit of suspicion was totally controlling Sammy, even affecting his work and certainly affecting his home life.

Sammy's wife persuaded him to attend two counseling sessions, then we set a date for his deliverance prayer session. However, before that date came, he bolted into our office and cried, "You have to pray for me now! I can't wait for my prayer date. Something is telling me to go home and kill my family, then myself." We instructed him to stay with his sister for the night, since we were not able to pray for him right at that moment.

The next morning Sammy came to our office for prayer. It was normally our day off, but we felt the urgency of the need and we were concerned for the welfare of his family.

During our prayer for Sammy, we called out a spirit of jealousy and suspicion, and immediately he began to manifest. Claire's hands were on his shoulders and the spirit tried to bite them, so she put her hands on his back. Then the spirit in him tried to bite his own arms and shoulders. At that point I commanded the spirit, "Don't you hurt him, in Jesus' Name!" The spirit began to rip his shirt from one shoulder to the other, and when the session was over, there was shirt fabric all over the floor. He left our office with little shreds of shirt hanging from his shoulders. But he left with a smile on his face, beaming from ear to ear because he was finally set free!

Sammy was thrilled to be free from the torment he had suffered for so long before his deliverance. We praise God every time we see His mercy and power set someone free.

Many times a demon in the husband knows exactly what to do or say to trigger a demon in the wife (and vice versa). Demons of anger, strife, argument and violence feed off each other. Whenever there is strife, those demons get fed their lunch; when they get hungry for dinner, they cause the couple to argue some more! You see, the couple's fighting just feeds the devils and empowers them to get bigger and stronger. QUIT ARGUING! Starve those demons! When you get rid of them through deliverance, the strife disappears and the marriage is healed.

For where envying and strife is, there is confusion and every work. (James 3:16)

LYING
I have seen also in the prophets of Jerusalem an horrible thing: they commit adultery, and walk in lies: they strengthen also the hands of evildoers, that none doth return from his wickedness:

74

they are all of them unto me as Sodom, and the inhabitants thereof as Gomorrah. (Jeremiah 23:14)

- Deception/Lies   II Thess. 2:10
- Exaggeration
- Profanity   I Tim. 4:7
- Hypocrisy
- Condemning Others
- Theft
- Isolation
- Vanity
- Adultery

Lying accompanies homosexual/lesbian spirits; in fact, there will be three stronghold spirits present: lying, whoredom, and perversion.

The spirit of lying not only causes persons to lie but lies *to them*, causing them to believe things that are not true. Many times this spirit will pretend it has left but it hasn't, and one of the common manifestations is laughter. Usually this spirit has to be called out many times before it actually leaves. The person will not look you in the eyes, and this is evidence of a deceptive spirit.

If a person has a tendency to exaggerate, this spirit sets him up for deeper involvement in deception. Routine questions about one's personal life intimidate the person into telling less truth and the spirit feeds on the individual's deception. The more the deception, the bigger the spirit becomes in that life. It's like the fictional Pinocchio: every time he told a lie, his nose grew bigger and bigger. Soon a person becomes so deceptive that the spirit of lying actually takes over. Some people jokingly call this "evangelistically speaking" but God calls it a deceptive spirit.

ACCOUNT

The spirit of lying often intermingles with the spirits of perversion and lust. A pastor of a large church once came to us seeking deliverance. He was in bondage to a spirit of deception intermingled with spirits of perversion and lust, and he had seduced many women in his congregation. He was a skillful deceiver and twisted the Word of God in such a way that he made the women believe that what they were doing was scriptural! The spirit of lying and deception had deceived him, as well.

This pastor was a handsome man who had an outgoing, charming personality. The spirit of deception had enabled him to walk in confidence, even arrogance, but when he came to us, he was humble and desperate to be free. He had come to recognize the terrible bondage he was living in and he wanted to be set free from his torment. After counseling and prayer for deliverance, God set him free from the spirits of lying, perversion and lust and he was totally restored. Today he walks in victory!

ANTI-CHRIST

And every spirit that confesseth not that Jesus Christ is come in the flesh is not of God: and this is that spirit of antichrist, whereof ye have heard that it should come; and even now already is it in the world. (I John 4:3)

- Doubt and Unbelief
- Rebellion
- Witchcraft
- Self-exaltation

This spirit always leaves angry and the people bound by this spirit generally are rebellious. The spirit of anti-Christ inhabits people who have been involved in witchcraft, and ungodly soul ties have to be broken with individuals in the past.

We see a lot of witchcraft in churches today and it is evident in people who have condemning or critical spirits who try to control within the church body. Because witchcraft is operating in churches, we need to pray for discerning of spirits to recognize this spirit, then take authority over it and bind it.

The motive of the spirit of anti-Christ is to destroy the Church—it is straight from the pit of hell. Satan himself is behind this spirit. It is imperative that these spirits of witchcraft, rebellion and accusation be kicked out of people's lives. They need to be replaced by a spirit of intercession to pray for our leaders and others in the Body of Christ. This action will fulfill God's purpose for the Church and for our lives.

ACCOUNT—Claire

Chung, a soft-spoken Korean man, had been a champion in martial arts since childhood; in fact, he came from a long line of champions. At the time he came to us, he was a black belt and a teacher of martial arts.

After his counseling sessions were completed, we told him we had set aside two hours for his deliverance session and he said quietly, "It will take much longer than that." Even though we were mildly surprised at that comment, we didn't attach too much importance to it. This man seemed very meek and shy, but later we found that he had told someone that he had a "dark side." He warned his friend that if that side of him ever showed up, the friend should get as far away from him as possible—and as quickly as possible!

In his prayer session, we came to see what he was talking about. As we do in all deliverance prayers, we commanded the part of his personality that was not "born again" to depart and nothing happened. We were aware that there were multi-personalities present but we knew from experience that until you discern them and can call them all by name, they will *hide*. It is extremely important to be specific concerning different personalities.

Chung sat in a chair, I stood behind him with my hands on his shoulders, and Paul sat across from Chung. Paul addressed the "warrior" personality—and it came forth like a LION. Chung began doing karate movements with his hands (even though Paul was holding onto his hands as tightly as he could), then he went straight for Paul's throat. As I watched this unfold, my faith level went down considerable and I began to get a little nervous. At other times when we have encountered an overpowering spirit getting out of control, I would summon a strong man to help us, but today no one was around.

When Chung went for Paul's throat, I began to call out Chung's name. Whenever a demon has taken over a person, calling out the name of the person usually gets them back to themselves. When I called Chung by name, Paul looked at me with wide eyes. "Don't do that! Let's get rid of this devil RIGHT NOW." Well in my opinion, "right now" wasn't looking too good to me, and I wanted to have Paul around a long time. Negative thoughts bombarded by mind.

I was wrestling with Chung, too, trying to hold him in his chair. Finally, I sat down beside him because we have found that spirits of rage, murder, violence, hatred and anger want you to fight with them. They will struggle with you and if you struggle back, they LOVE IT. Your struggle feeds and empowers them. However, if you take your hands off the person, that spirit will usually stop manifesting—and that is exactly what happened.

I tried to talk to Chung and discovered that I was speaking to the devil that had taken control of him. Since the spirit knew that he was not going to get anywhere with Paul because Paul never once felt fear or doubt, he decided to direct his attention to me. The spirit tried to intimidate me and told me that it would kill me; then he asked me if I would like him to show me *how* he would kill me.

I was looking directly into Chung's eyes as I conversed with the spirit and to my utter surprise, the pupil in the middle of his eye (the little black circle) turned milky white and grew to about twice its normal size. I was so fascinated with that "white pupil" that I didn't look into the other eye to see if the same thing was happening. I had never seen anything like this before! I kept talking, but my mind was asking, "What in the world is going on here?"

Suddenly Chung's mouth turned into a sneer and he was staring at me with that strange eye! I kept calling Chung's name, hoping he would come back to himself. I verbally agreed with him that he could kill and that he could probably kill multiple persons. Then I warned him that if he killed someone, he would go to prison. A point of clarification here: a warrior spirit deludes a person into thinking that it (the spirit) will be his protection forever. But warrior spirits have spoken to us and told us that they do not like prison and will not go with a person into prison. The spirits simply go into someone else.

I continued to try to reason with Chung, telling him that the warrior spirit wanted to kill him, that it hated him and one day would take him over if he did not get rid of it. I also warned Chung that he could end up hurting or killing someone he loved. I explained thoroughly (again) that God is the power that does the work of deliverance and he, Chung, must be willing to let it happen.

Paul and I are *nothing* but vessels to be used of God to speak forth His authority to make the demons leave a person. We again explained to Chung that if he wanted to hang on to this spirit, it would never leave him. I knew in my spirit that this demon was trying to convince Chung to let it stay. And the demon was going back to its old argument that Chung needed it for protection. The same old lie.

I explained again to Chung that the warrior spirit was there for evil purposes (to kill, steal and destroy). I tried to convince him that the Spirit of God in him (Chung) had all power and authority to protect him. God is our ultimate protection over satan and his kingdom.

The battle was being waged in Chung. Again he snarled at Paul, growled loudly, and pointed toward a picture of the Lion of Judah hanging on our wall. The picture shows the pierced paws of the lion, and as Chung pointed, he said, "I was the one who drove the nails in Jesus' hands and I'm going to drive them in your hands, too."

I reached for a bottle of anointing oil that was sitting on the desk. We had prayed over this oil and asked God to make it a symbol of the blood that Jesus had shed on Calvary. As soon as I poured some on Chung's head *the demon went crazy*. Chung broke his hands free from Paul and grabbed his own head. When he got the oil on his hands, he began to shake them so violently that we were afraid he would hurt himself. It seemed like he would shake his hands completely off.

But here's the miracle! That warrior personality left through his hands and he almost collapsed, closing his eyes and bowing his head for quite some time. He stayed bowed in a posture of reverence to the Lord of Lords and King of Kings because the Lord had just proven Himself *all powerful over the forces of satan* and his kingdom. And Chung was right; it took more than two hours for him to be completely set free from all the evil baggage that he had picked up over the years.

Two weeks later we had the pleasure and joy of seeing Chung in a church service, kneeling before the Lord, tears streaming down his face, worshiping the God of all power and creation!

Interestingly, we have had two demon spirits speak to us and brag that they were responsible for driving the nails in Jesus and piercing His side. We believe that all satan's kingdom was there at the crucifixion and probably most of them resided in the Roman soldiers!

ACCOUNT—Demons Were Part of His Household

Andy was an athletic high school student, muscular and handsome with curly brown hair. Upon meeting this young man, we immediately discerned that he was under great demonic oppression. The demons would get especially angry when he was close to the anointing, as when he attended a church service where the power of God was flowing.

Andy had given his heart to the Lord and truly wanted to live completely for Christ, but these demonic strongholds held him back. He knew he needed help, so he came to us. His mother was into occult practices and, in fact, had dedicated a room in their home to satan. Strange things happened in that room and Andy told us that when he entered it, a power like electricity flowed through his body.

Andy knew that four demons lived in his house and he knew them well. He told us their names and described how they dressed. Omar was a swordsman; Nye was a martial arts expert; Omdropolis was strong, old, wise, and had a beard; and Caisha dressed in a warrior's outfit.

On Andy's day to be prayed for, he was delayed and he actually had to walk several miles in the heat of the day to make his appointment. But he was very determined to be set free!

In our session with Andy, we broke all the soul ties between him and the demons living in his house. During this prayer, he literally went crazy and power rose up in him like a gorilla. The demons were enraged, but one by one we called them out by name. Satan's kingdom loses and Christ wins, because He won the victory on the cross two thousand years ago. All we have to do is BELIEVE IT AND USE THE AUTHORITY HE HAS GIVEN TO US.

One of satan's best tools in keeping Christians bound is to keep them from realizing the authority they have within themselves through Jesus Christ. Satan knows that when we realize that the God who created him and his kingdom now lives in us, and we get hold of the truth that satan has to bow to that authority, he (satan) is under our feet!

Andy was gloriously delivered that day because he took hold of the wonderful truth of his victory in Jesus Christ!

POVERTY

The thief cometh not, but for to steal, and to kill, and to destroy: I am come that they might have life, and that they might have it more abundantly. (John 10:10)

The spirit of poverty steals your time, your money, your spiritual growth, your love, your peace, and your joy. People can receive large amounts of money and even have excellent jobs, but this demon devours their money like it is water running through a strainer. If you are plagued with this spirit, you will notice various symptoms in your life. Your car will often break down and there will be things happening around your house that constantly "steal" your money.

The spirit of poverty usually comes through the inherited bloodline, or an ungodly soul tie that has developed in your past. Just because your parents were poor does not mean that you need to be poor. If you see that your grandparents were poor, then your parents were poor, and now you are poor, there could be a spirit of poverty being passed down from generation to generation. This curse of poverty can be broken because Jesus took the curse for us. We must take authority over this spirit and tell it to leave in Jesus' Name.

You can also bring a curse of poverty upon yourself if you do not pay tithes as is required in Malachi 3:9: *Ye are cursed with a curse: for ye have robbed me, even this whole nation.*

Bring ye all the tithes into the storehouse, that there may be meat in mine house, and prove me now herewith, saith the Lord of hosts, if I will not open you the windows of heaven, and pour you out a blessing, that there shall not be room enough to receive it. (Malachi 3:10)

If we are following the scriptures by tithing, the spirit of poverty can be kicked out of our lives, making us candidates to receive God's blessings.

Broken vows also can open doors to allow poverty to enter. If you entered into a contract to buy something and then claimed bankruptcy without paying that debt, you must confess and ask God to forgive you and set you free from any bondage of poverty.

ACCOUNT

A leading church in Tampa, Florida, had a quarterly seminar on inner-city ministry for pastors and church leaders from across the nation. Our deliverance sessions were being offered in this seminar, as well, and at the end of each session people were invited to come for deliverance.

During such a session, as we prayed for a lady named Edith, the Lord told us to call out a spirit of poverty. In obedience to God's instruction, we did so, and Edith began to manifest by wrapping her arms tightly around herself and turning sideways, pressing her lips together very tightly. We continued to call out the spirit of poverty and suddenly, there was an explosive sound of air and the spirit left through her mouth with tremendous force.

After the deliverance she shared with us that she had inherited large sums of money five different times in her lifetime. Each time the money would disappear because of bad investments or bad judgment on her part. In each case, satan stole the money from her and she definitely had a spirit of poverty over her life! But that day, thank God, she was completely set free!

BONDAGE

For ye have not received the spirit of bondage again to fear; but ye have received the spirit of adoption, whereby we cry, Abba, Father. (Romans 8:15)

- Hindering (can't call on God)
- (Hold back God's call on your life)
- Greed
- Gluttony
- Obesity
- Addiction (drugs, alcohol, nicotine)
- Bulimia
- Anorexia
- Poverty

If you love God and have a deep desire to be all that He wants you to be, yet it seems you fall short, you need to suspect that you have a hindering spirit operating in your life. These spirits do tremendous harm to the Body of Christ. Addiction of any kind, whether to alcohol, nicotine, drugs (even prescription drugs) and food, will hold you in bondage. This bondage is like a person wrapped in heavy chains and we have discovered that satan usually uses this spirit on those who have the most potential to do God's work. However, once they are set free, they become absolute powerhouses for the Lord!

ACCOUNT

A woman who had been bound by the spirit of addiction to nicotine since she was twelve years old came to us for deliverance. She had planned to come to us on several previous occasions, but this spirit hindered her coming.

The day she made it to the session, the spirits of bondage and addiction were so strong that they made her want to leave. Finally, she announced loudly, "I have to go out and take a smoke!" We had been praying for approximately two hours and the spirit could not stand to be in the presence of the Lord any longer, so she left right in the middle of the deliverance session.

Although she said she wanted to go for a smoke, we were afraid we would not see her again. However, she surprised us and returned and let us pray for her. She had done her assignments from previous sessions and she desperately wanted the spirit to leave. We called out the spirit of bondage that bound her, but the spirit was really determined not to leave. After a manifestation and protest, we commanded the spirit to leave, in Jesus' Name, and she was completely set free from hindering spirits and addiction to nicotine.

The following week we got a telephone call from this lady that we found a little amusing. She was very upset and told us, "You didn't tell me I was going to have to get a new car! Ever since my deliverance from the spirit of nicotine, the smell in my car makes me almost ill. All I can smell in my car is smoke! And when I go in the house, all I can smell is smoke in my closet, on my furniture and in my clothes. It's awful."

She had absolutely no withdrawal symptoms, because that spirit had completely left her. We have noticed that when people are set free from the spirit of addiction, they have no withdrawal symptoms. They are totally set free! Praise God!

INFIRMITY

And, behold, there was a woman which had a spirit of infirmity eighteen years, and was bowed together, and could in no wise lift up herself. (Luke 13:11)

- Inherited curse (infirmity)
- Arthritis
- Asthma/hay fever/ allergies
- Fever
- Cancer
- Death
- Every disease
- Pain

We have had many marvelous healings occur in our office. Quite often people come to us who have prayed continuously for their healing and, almost out of desperation, they find themselves begging God for healing. When they get no results, they seek out pastors and evangelists to lay hands on them, hoping that maybe, just maybe, this time they will be healed! It is sad, but true, that many times, after all their efforts—still nothing happens. However, when they go through our deliverance program, they receive their healing.

Why is this true? It certainly is not because our program is any better than any other ministry and it definitely is not because we have more power in ourselves. The answer is quite simple: If the devil (i.e., a spirit of infirmity) has a legal right to be there, he is not going to leave until he gets kicked out. That infirmity could be there because of an ungodly soul tie, or because of sin, or it could possibly be a familiar spirit that came down through the inherited bloodline. If any of this is the case, before the healing will be able to take place, you need to get rid of the spirit of infirmity that is causing the illness.

We believe that is why the "signs" of the believer are listed in a particular order—**cast out . . . lay hands** (see Mark 16:17). Of course, not all infirmities are demonic; some conditions are caused by accidents. For instance, if a person gets a hard hit on the head by a baseball, or a bat, or in a car accident, he may have resultant epileptic seizures. Of course, this person can be healed through prayer, but it is a physical healing only. But if an infirmity is caused by a demonic power, such as a generational curse, get rid of the spirit and speak God's healing into the situation.

ACCOUNT

Esther, a loving, concerned grandmother, came to us with an alarming story regarding her granddaughter. She related that approximately two years earlier, her granddaughter had fallen into a lake and had nearly drowned. Paramedics were able to revive her, but she had been in a coma ever since. Esther had legal custody of the child and asked if we would pray for her.

We went to the hospital and saw a fragile, delicate little girl lying in a coma, still and silent, unable to move in any way. Her tiny arms, hands, legs and feet were twisted, an obvious symptom of her condition, but she was also blind, a not-so-obvious symptom. Our hearts were stricken as we looked at her and we knew it was time to proceed.

The first step in deliverance is counseling and we counsel with the parents or guardian (the covering) of a child under the age of accountability. In this case, we counseled with Esther and discovered that both her mother and sister had drowned in separate accidents. It was evident to us that drowning was a curse on this family.

During the deliverance prayer session, we prayed for the granddaughter with her grandmother sitting in proxy for her. There were no manifestations whatsoever as we prayed for *Esther*. But when we laid hands on Esther and *prayed for her granddaughter*, commanding the spirits to leave the child (through the grandmother), the spirits got violent. Esther began to look and act like a mad dog! She actually showed her teeth and started biting at the air.

When we called out a spirit of death and a curse of infirmity, the demons shook Esther like a rag whipping in the wind! They put up a tremendous resistance to leaving. We called out every single spirit by the medical name of the child's infirmities, and each one reacted when its name was called. Esther was exhausted by the time we finished, but her granddaughter was set free from the spirits of infirmity through the love and faith of her concerned grandmother.

We saw Esther a week later and she told us that her granddaughter was not only responding, but was communicating. The hospital personnel were excited and shocked, but Esther told them that God had done this miracle!

Not all infirmities and sicknesses are demonic, but this one definitely was!

WHOREDOM

My people ask counsel at their stocks, and their staff declareth unto them: for the spirit of whoredoms hath caused them to err, and they have gone a whoring from under their God. (Hosea 4:12)

- Prostitution
- Martial Arts
- Cults
- Religious
- Legalism
- Idolatry (money, etc.)
- Emotional Weakness
- Fornication   Ez. 16:15
- Adultery   Gal. 5:19

We save the spirits of whoredom and perversion until last to pray for because almost everyone has them. By saving them to the last, they have lost their strength, because there is nothing left for them to cling to. Their friends are gone!

Spirits of religion, legalism and cults manifest by trying to get you to believe they know it all, that they are right and you are wrong. Spirits speak forth and tell you that the deliverance isn't happening and that you are doing it wrong. They might even try to talk you out of doing deliverance. The homosexual and lesbian spirits have three stronghold spirits over them: **lying, whoredom, and pervesion**. When praying for these spirits, we bind the strong man and spoil his house. After these three ruling spirits are gone, we find that the spirits of homosexuality and lesbianism are not that strong, and they leave quickly when you call them out in Jesus' Name.

Do you continually find yourself falling into fornication and adultery? If so, there is a good possibility that you have a spirit of emotional weakness. This spirit can be dealt with by simply breaking ungodly soul ties with people you have had relationships with in the past. By calling out the spirit of emotional weakness, the spirit will go and a person will have the ability and strength to say "NO" to sin.

ACCOUNT

Mary Jane was a flamboyant lady who always "made an entrance" wherever she showed up (and she showed up at churches all over town). She always arrived late, wearing the most ostentatious attire one could imagine. Her jewelry was bright and flashy and, coupled with her tasteless clothing and big hats, served merely to make her appear almost pathetic. She made it a point to leave a service at least a couple of times, distracting those around her. She also would loudly shout "Amen" at times, drawing even more attention to herself.

If the Holy Spirit moved in a service, Mary Jane would often go into a frenzy, but Paul and I knew that she was not responding to the Holy Spirit but, rather, to demonic forces. We have found that this type of thing happens often in church services where the Holy Spirit is moving. The manifested presence of God will stir up demonic spirits in people. Without the discernment of the Holy Spirit, you might actually think these people are very spiritual.

Mary Jane had an answer for everything and would dominate a conversation, pretending to be an expert on any subject being discussed, especially religion.

When Mary Jane asked to see us, we jumped for joy. One of her friends had been through our program and had highly recommended it to her. We discerned that she had a problem with religion/legalism, although she thought she was just depressed.

After receiving teaching and counseling in our sessions, Mary Jane realized that she had many strongholds in her life, so she prepared herself for deliverance by fasting and praying. Mary Jane was gloriously delivered from the spirit of religion/legalism and now she is no longer a spectacle. Her deliverance enabled her to use taste and discretion in her appearance and behavior.

PERVERSION

Whoso walketh uprightly shall be saved: but he that is perverse in his ways shall fall at once. (Prov. 28:18)

- Word Twisting   Acts 13:10
- Lust   Prov. 23:33
- Lesbianism
- Homosexuality
- Masturbation
- Sodomy
- Bestiality
- Child Molestation
- Incest
- Exhibitionism
- Pornography
- Seducing Spirit   I Tim. 4:1

Has perversion sunk its deadly claws into you? Are you being tormented with lust? If you answer "yes" to either of these questions, do not be embarrassed—just join a huge crowd. We take this stronghold very seriously because this spirit is so powerful in today's world that you are being set up by the devil almost everywhere you look!

Lust and perversion can gain entrance into your life in many ways. In the majority of cases we have dealt with, we have found that they have come in through familiar spirits passed down through the inherited bloodline. Either that, or they have come in because of childhood molestation. No matter how they enter, you are strongly influenced to commit deliberate sin.

Molestation of an innocent child opens a door for lust and perversion to enter. They do not want it; it was not their sin or their fault, but it gives satan and his kingdom a legal right to enter the child. This is why countless teenagers find themselves being promiscuous without understanding their actions, not realizing that the prior molestation opened the door to lust and perversion in their lives. They may feel in their hearts that something is not right, but they just brush aside those thoughts, assuming that they are just "being normal." Sadly, we live in a society that teaches them that their behavior *is* normal, even if they ask for help. They are told it is all right to "explore" and if it feels good, do it! Many innocent victims are being consoled while blindly walking down the path of destruction.

It is important to know that all evil spirits are lustful and hungry and need to be fed. Every time you do a perverted act of any kind, you are feeding that spirit and it grows. This spirit can begin its hold on a person through pornography, but believe me, it doesn't stay there! After a while merely looking at pictures will not satisfy the spirit of pornography. A person goes on to the next level of lust and perversion, and after experiencing several levels, they may progress to the final level, which is rape and murder. We have ministered to many people who have reached this level in their thought life and they come to us, knowing they are out of control. The assignment of all evil spirits is to steal, kill and destroy. Even spirits of perversion will mature to this level if you keep feeding them.

There is a lot of teaching today that states, "Whatever goes on between a husband and wife behind closed doors is okay." This is a lie straight from the pits of hell! No perversion will ever stay behind a closed door. One (or both) of those partners will take it outside eventually. You see, when you stir up those spirits, they are not satisfied to stay "behind closed doors" at that level. If you are looking at pornography with your spouse, or doing any other perverted thing, you are shaking hands with the devil and he will bite your arm off!

During deliverance, these particular spirits manifest in various ways: a spirit of masturbation usually comes out through the hands; oral sex will manifest by contorting the person's mouth. Over half the time, spirits of perversion manifest by the persons sticking out their tongue like a snake, or licking their lips and becoming very seductive. Some have even slithered on the floor like a snake. When we are doing group sessions, we separate the men and women and pray privately for these particular spirits. And we instruct the demons not to manifest themselves.

Twisting God's Word around to say what you want is a form of perversion. We have found this extremely common in religious leaders in the church who want to seduce women.

ACCOUNT—Pastors In Bondage

Many, many pastors from all different denominations are controlled by demonic strongholds of lust and perversion and come to us for counsel. This is certainly an indication that satan will snare anyone in any profession!

We had three pastors come to us in three consecutive weeks because of their obsession with homosexuality. They absolutely hated what they were doing but had an undying drive that was just as cruel and relentless as that of a heroin addict.

These pastors, all truly devoted to God with a deep love for the Lord, had the doors of lust opened to them when they were small children. They had all been sexually molested.

A pastor came to us who was sexually active with many women other than his wife. He testified that as a child he had been introduced to extremely grotesque, perverted acts by his little friends—the sons of his pastor and head deacon.

Another pastor came to us but never mentioned any problems of homosexuality. However, as we began praying for him, a female voice spoke through him. We immediately knew what his problem was, and called out the "feminine" personality.

These are only a few examples of pastors we have prayed for. Satan and his cohorts don't care who you are or what you do. If they can entrap you, they will! Their aim is destruction. If you are a pastor, priest, or evangelist, and are being tormented by lust or perversion, you need to know that you can be set free! Demons are rude guests and they won't leave until they are kicked out. So kick them out, in Jesus' Name, and you won't have to live in bondage anymore!

ACCOUNT—Pastors' Mass Deliverance

A church we attended had periodic training conferences for pastors, associate pastors, and leaders from across the nation. We were allowed to offer a teaching class on deliverance to those who were interested and some gave up their lunch break to attend.

During the class we distributed a list of Stronghold Forces and all the demons that they have rule over. After carefully reading this list, one of the pastors told us that he had every stronghold on the list. We could tell that this came as a shock to him—but not to us, as we have heard this comment before.

As the class continued, people began to ask if they could do a "self-deliverance." We explained that sometimes spirits are so deep-seated that you really need some additional prayer power to help. Also, if you have a deceiving spirit, it will not let you know what demonic influence is present. Consequently, they unanimously decided to return that evening for a mass deliverance. This was going to be a FIRST for us, but we knew that the Holy Spirit would take over, no matter what we had in mind or planned.

The evening flowed from beginning to end with great freedom in the air. At one point, a problem arose with a demon, but a spontaneous group singing about the blood of Jesus put an end to that! The people bonded with such unity that whenever a demon would manifest, all of them would lay on hands and pray for the individual in bondage. It seemed like everything that *could* happen during a deliverance session *did*. Demons spoke through people, people got violent, some laughed and some cried. It was truly a "hands on" teaching—with life-changing results.

The following week we received a number of phone calls from people with reports that lives had been changed and they were walking in more freedom than they had ever dreamed possible. One pastor shared with us that when he preached his next sermon, he experienced more anointing than he had ever known.

NOTE: Pastors, please be aware that these spirits will hold back the calling of God on your life. It is their job! And they will not *quit*—they need to be *fired*!

ACCOUNT—Paul

We need to preface this account by confessing that sometimes we are quite taken aback by what the demonic kingdom can do to a person in the physical realm.

We were praying deliverance for a young man, Francis, who had practiced homosexuality for as long as he could remember. As in the case of most, he had been sexually abused as a very young boy. As we continued in his deliverance, we witnessed something quite out of the ordinary. While we were praying for him, Francis suddenly became blind! As strange as it may seem, not only could he not see, but his eyes were "milky" from a white film over them.

Then, to top things off, he began slipping in and out of a trance-like state and, frankly, this was quite frightening to Claire, because we were unable to bring him out of it. He was absolutely panic-stricken. Every time he would snap out of his trance, he would go into hysterics, screaming at the top of his lungs, "I'M BLIND! I'M BLIND!"

After about twenty minutes, Francis calmed down and told us that he actually felt the demons leave him through his eyes. We then realized that the demons had gained their legal right to be there through the "lust of the eye." But they had lost that right and reluctantly made their exit. There is no doubt that the demons put Francis through a frightful experience (and caused us some anxiety, as well), but the outcome was GLORIOUS! Not only did Francis' eyesight return, but he was also totally and completely set free.

Many times a demon spirit will cause pain when it leaves a person, but this was the first time we had ever seen a person go completely blind. People who have experienced pain during deliverance have told us that the pain only lasted for a few moments. Our guess is that the demons are so furious over losing custody of their home that they don't know what to do, so they throw a temper tantrum on their way out.

8

Are You Cursed?

Are You Cursed?

We have observed three types of curses: inherited curses, self-imposed curses, and curses that have come from someone in the occult. Let us discuss inherited curses first. These curses have taproots such as poverty, sickness, disease, abuse, and many other things that have come from the inherited bloodline.

Thou shalt not bow down thyself to them, nor serve them: for I the Lord thy God am a jealous God, visiting the iniquity of the fathers upon the children unto the third and fourth generation of them that hate me ... (Exodus 20:5)

GENERATIONAL CURSES
Generational curses are things that we as individuals can inherit from our parents. If the parents are in poverty, many times children will also live in poverty. If there is sugar diabetes in the inherited bloodline, that curse can flow down from generation to generation. If the grandmother has migraine headaches, we have seen that same curse flow down to the mother, then on down to the granddaughter. The spirit of infirmity flows from generation to generation.

Likewise, if there is sexual abuse in the family, it will continue through the inherited line from generation to generation. It is a curse that is inherited and it comes down three and four generations. So many curses can be passed on through the bloodline: addiction, alcoholism, many illnesses and bondages.

The good news is that a generational curse can be broken! Whether it is inherited or received in another manner, it can be broken by you! You, as an individual, need to confess your sins and ask God to forgive you. Then confess the sins of your forefathers (Lev. 26:40-42). What we mean is, you can simply agree with God that they have sinned. Then you need to break the ungodly soul ties between you and your parents and their ancestral line.

In addition to the above, you can break the power of that specific curse and, as a born-again Christian, you have the power and

95

authority to break the effect of that curse over your life and that of your children (or any future children you may have) in Jesus' Name. You can be set free of curses because of what Jesus did for us on Calvary.

SELF-IMPOSED CURSES

In addition to inherited generational curses, there are self-imposed curses. You can bring curses upon yourself just by the things you do. Listed below are some causes of self-imposed curses:

1. Non-tither. If you are a born-again Christian and a non-tither, you can bring a curse upon yourself by disobeying God's laws.
2. Legalism
3. Theft
4. Perjury
5. Judgmentalism
6. Accusation
7. Taking offense
8. By the words you speak

These actions bring self-imposed curses upon your life.

We live in two separate worlds: the physical world and the spiritual world. The physical world is visible to us at all times, but the spiritual world is invisible. Hence, we live in the spiritual world by *faith*. As we increase our faith, we become stronger and more powerful in the spiritual world.

For we wrestle not against flesh and blood, but against principalities, against powers, against the rulers of the darkness of this world, against spiritual wickedness in high places. (Eph. 6:12)

The battles we fight are in the spiritual realm, not the physical, although the *manifestations* are in the physical realm. For instance, healing comes from the Holy Spirit but we see the healing in the physical realm.

There is also a spirit behind a curse, whether inherited or self-imposed. An evil spirit brings the curse.

If you have a business failure, there could be an evil spirit behind the problem. If you have problems in your household through disharmony or even divorce, there is probably an evil spirit behind the problem. If your children are rebelling, a spirit is behind that rebellion. There are evil spirits behind strife, division, and rebellion.

In the Old Testament, Joshua had a promise from God that he would enter the Promised Land, but Joshua had to go into battle to possess the promise. There was warfare involved!

Blessed be the God and Father of our Lord Jesus Christ, who hath blessed us with all spiritual blessings in heavenly places in Christ. (Eph. 1:3)

You see, the blessings of God are there for us, but we need to pray to receive the blessings!

Christ hath redeemed us from the curse of the law, being made a curse for us: for it is written, Cursed is every one that hangeth on a tree: that the blessing of Abraham might come on the Gentiles through Jesus Christ; that we might receive the promise of the Spirit through faith. (Gal. 3:13, 14)

We have the promise of being free from the curse, but we have to "go into warfare" in order to receive that promise. The curse is there either because of sin from our ancestral line, or our own sin. But we can be free!

Yes, we can receive freedom from the curse through faith, but we have to fight in the spirit realm. Just because you are *born* does not mean that you are automatically *born again*. No, you have to pray, believe, and receive salvation. As a Christian, we do not automatically become healed; we must go to God in prayer and ask for healing, then appropriate it.

This same principle applies to receiving freedom and deliverance from a curse. *Appropriation* is necessary in order to break the power of a curse. We need to ask God to protect us and live in us, then we can go into spiritual warfare and receive our freedom from the power of the curse.

BLESSINGS
Deuteronomy 28:1-14 outlines ten different blessings and Christ made it possible for the blessings to flow down through the generations since Abraham.

1. **We will be exalted**.

And it shall come to pass, if thou shalt hearken diligently unto the voice of the Lord thy God, to observe and to do all his commandments which I command thee this day, that the Lord thy God will set thee on high above all nations of the earth. (Deut. 28:1)

2. **We will be promoted**.

And all these blessings shall come on thee, and overtake thee, if thou shalt hearken unto the voice of the Lord thy God. (Deut. 28:2)

Blessed shalt thou be in the city, and blessed shalt thou be in the field. (Deut. 28:3)

3. **We will have health**.

Blessed shall be the fruit of thy body, and the fruit of thy ground, and the fruit of thy cattle, the increase of thy kine, and the flocks of thy sheep. (Deut. 28:4)

4. **We will have prosperity**.

Blessed shall be thy basket and thy store. (Deut. 28:5)

5. **We will be redeemed**.

Blessed shalt thou be when thou comest in, and blessed shalt thou be when thou goest out. (Deut. 28:6)

6. **We will have victory**.

The Lord shall cause thine enemies that rise up against thee to be smitten before thy face: they shall come out against thee one way, and flee before thee seven ways. (Deut. 28:7)

7. **We will be fruitful**.

The Lord shall command the blessing upon thee in thy storehouses, and in all that thou settest thine hand unto; and he shall bless thee in the land which the Lord thy God giveth thee. (Deut. 28:8)

8. **We will be successful**.

The Lord shall establish thee an holy people unto himself, as he hath sworn unto thee, if thou shalt keep the commandments of the Lord thy God, and walk in his ways.(Deut. 28:9)

9. **We will have creative ability**.

And all people of the earth shall see that thou art called by the name of the Lord; and they shall be afraid of thee. (Deut. 28:10) And the Lord shall make thee plenteous in goods, in the fruit of thy body, and in the fruit of thy cattle, and in the fruit of thy ground, in the land which the Lord sware unto thy fathers to give thee. (Deut. 28:11)

10. **We will have abundance**.
The Lord shall open unto thee his good treasure, the heaven to give the rain unto thy land in his season, and to bless all the work of thine hand: and thou shalt lend unto many nations, and thou shalt not borrow. (Deut. 28:12)

And the Lord shall make thee the head, and not the tail; and thou shalt be above only, and thou shalt not be beneath; if that thou hearken unto the commandments of the Lord thy God, which I command thee this day, to observe and to do them. (Deut. 28:13)

And thou shalt not go aside from any of the words which I command thee this day, to the right hand, or to the left, to go after other gods to serve them. (Deut. 28:14)

I receive these blessings in the Name of Jesus. I want the blessings that God has for me. I want blessings to be a part of my life!

CURSES
The Bible speaks about curses in Deuteronomy 28:15-44. There could be many symptoms of curses in your own life and we want to mention a few in order to help you identify them.

1. **Humiliation**

2. **Barrenness**

3. **Limitations**
Do you find yourself always facing limitations in your life?

4. **Unfruitfulness**
Do you find that you cannot be fruitful?

5. **Failure or Defeat**

6. **Constant Sickness**
Are you or another family member always sick?

7. **Mental and Emotional Pressure**
This mental and emotional pressure could be from everyday life, but is it always there?

8. **Family Stress and Breakdown**
   Satan attacks the family, especially in the area of divorce.

9. **Oppression and Depression**
   Many people are living in depression to the point of near suicide. This could be a curse!

10. **Fear or Torment**
    Do you find that you cannot sleep at night because of being racked with fear and torment? Or do you sleep too much, not wanting to face the world?

11. **Insanity**

12. **Constant Debt**

13. **Sickness that will not respond to medical treatment.**
    This unresolved sickness is nothing but a curse upon your life and you can be FREE OF IT!

14. **Miscarriages**

15. **Accident Prone**
    Are you often involved in accidents? Do you constantly drop things? Are you always falling?

16. **Suicide**

17. **Poverty and Financial Pressures**

If you are experiencing one or more of the above symptoms, then chances are YOU HAVE A CURSE UPON YOUR LIFE. But you can be set free of these curses.

As the bird by wandering, as the swallow by flying, so the curse causeless shall not come. (Prov. 26:2)

This scripture means that if you have a curse upon your life, there is a reason for it. It could be inherited or it could be self-imposed. It could even be a curse that someone in the occult put on you.

We want to help you understand why some of these curses may have come into your life so that you will be able to close those doors.

One open door that can allow a curse into your life is the occult world: for example, psychic healing, table tipping, mind control, and astral projection. Dabbling in such things can bring curses upon your life, because they deal with the occult world. Also, there are curses that have to do with revelation, astrology, automatic writing, hearing voices, crystal balls, fortune tellers, palm reading, foot reading, channeling, clairvoyance, and New Age practices. Taking certain pledges and oaths can also bring curses into your being.

Thou shalt make no covenant with them, nor with their gods. (Ex. 23:32)

We are not to worship other gods or get information or help from satan's kingdom in any way, shape or form. Ouija boards, crystals and much rock music also involve the occult.

Many people have traveled to other countries, in particular India, China, and Japan, and brought back little trinkets that they think are innocent. However, they have really brought back idols and gods of those countries. You see, spirits attach themselves to these trinkets and you could actually be bringing a curse into your home without being aware of it. Do not be deceived by these nice-looking ornaments!

Pornography and obscene pictures or literature in your home can also bring demonic curses upon you. We have to be extremely cautious about what we allow in our homes.

Our own words can be used to impose curses upon ourselves. The Word of God tells us in *Prov. 6:2 (NIV)*: *You have been trapped by what you have said and ensnared by the words of your mouth.*

Consider the story of the twelve spies who came back and reported to Moses. Ten of them said, "No, we cannot go into the promised land," and they didn't, because they spoke a curse upon themselves. However, two of them said, "We *can* go into the promised land." They spoke a blessing upon themselves and they *did* go into Canaan.

You can easily self-impose curses upon yourself by the words you speak, many times without even realizing it. If you say things like, "I'm clumsy; I'm bound to get the flu; it runs in my family; over my dead body; you're driving me crazy," you are speaking curses on yourself. All these seemingly innocuous little comments can bring a curse upon you.

We need to repent and revoke and renounce these things! Replace them with the blessings of God.

CURSES AGAINST YOU FROM OTHERS

Others can also speak curses upon you, if you allow them to work in your life. Words of manipulation, self-pity, control, failure and even death can bring a curse. But you do not have to receive negative words or comments or curses and accept them into your life. You can renounce them the minute you have knowledge of them.

No weapon that is formed against thee shall prosper; and every tongue that shall rise against thee in judgment thou shalt condemn. This is the heritage of the servants of the Lord, and their righteousness is of me, saith the Lord. (Isaiah 54:17)

The Bible says that as born-again children of God, we "shall speak forth" and condemn the words that are spoken against us. We have His power and authority in our lives and a curse cannot light on us unless we open the door for it. However, we must constantly be cautious to speak only blessings upon our own lives and the lives of others. Do not do anything to bring a curse upon yourself. When we are led by the Holy Spirit, we are justified by our words. Likewise, we can be condemned by our words. Why? Because words can activate a "spirit" of life or death. What do you choose to speak? Life or death? You have to make a choice!

Be careful what you speak to your children! Don't tell your children that they will never amount to anything. Choose to speak life and blessings upon them rather than curses.

Speak the power of God and divine health upon the lives of your children. *Speak these blessings over your children*: creativity, clarity, wisdom, righteousness and truthfulness. By doing this, your children will be a blessing to you and others. Remember that there is much power in the tongue, and be careful not to speak negative things over your children. Curses can only bring destruction.

OCCULT CURSES

Today, many people practice witchcraft, satanism, and voodoo. We do not always recognize these people-they could be at your job or even in your church. Witches are assigned to churches and given a mandate to destroy from within. And, as farfetched as this may sound, you need to be aware that your children's friends can be instruments of satan to bring a curse upon your entire family. In recent years, we have counseled people who have experienced all the above.

Why would someone do such a thing? It could be because they just do not like you, and want to hurt you or get rid of you for some reason. It could also be that you have hurt someone in the past and they want to get even with you. If you are having continued unexplained problems, you might want to take an inventory of who doesn't like you and then do a self-examination to try to find the reason:

1. Are you born again? Is Jesus lord of your life?
2. Is there sin in your life?
3. Are you judging, condemning, accusing, and gossiping about others?
4. Do you fear a curse? Fear can open a door to allow the curse to operate.

See if you need to break a soul tie between you and whomever you suspect of doing this to you. Put a Jesus bloodline between the two of you and break the curse in the Name of Jesus and cancel its assignment.

If you are under a curse, you do not have to remain there. If you have a curse that has been transferred to you through the inherited bloodline, you can break the ungodly soul tie between you and your inherited bloodline. Confess your sins and the sins of your forefathers and ask God to forgive you. Then you can break the power of the curse on your life! It will be miraculously lifted off of you and your entire household!

If you have spoken curses upon yourself, all you have to do is repent and ask God to forgive you, renouncing what you have spoken. Then resist the devil!

Submit yourselves therefore to God. Resist the devil, and he will flee from you. (James 4:7)

Replace negative words with the Word of God upon you and your children. You will find that blessings will overtake you and curses will end.

God wants you to have blessings upon your life—that is why Jesus died on the cross! He took the curse for us, but we have to appropriate His promise. We have a promise of freedom from the curse, but in order to receive possession of that promise, we may have to go into spiritual warfare (just like Joshua did).

God wants you to be free from the power of the curse and be blessed! He will do all this for you if you will just appropriate His promises in the Name of Jesus!

Daily Prayers

Daily Prayers

Evening, and morning, and at noon, will I pray, and cry aloud: and he shall hear my voice. (Psalm 55:17)

Paul and I cannot stress enough the importance of each person praying daily, in the morning, before you begin your day. We have included a "Daily Warfare Prayer" for you to follow.

David prayed the following prayer in II Samuel 7:27-29:

For thou, O Lord of hosts, God of Israel, hast revealed to thy servant, saying, I will build thee an house: therefore hath thy servant found in his heart to pray this prayer unto thee. And now, O Lord God, thou art that God, and thy words be true, and thou hast promised this goodness unto thy servant: therefore now let it please thee to bless the house of thy servant, that it may continue for ever before thee; for thou, O Lord God, hast spoken it: and with thy blessing let the house of thy servant be blessed for ever.

DAILY WARFARE PRAYER

Begin with praise and thanksgiving, then continue.

Heavenly Father, I come to you in the Name of Jesus, and I ask you to forgive me of anything I have done that could displease you in any way. I ask you to cover me with the blood of Jesus and fill me with your Holy Spirit. Cause my thoughts to be your thoughts, my desires your desires, my will your will, and put a guard across my mouth that I can say no more or no less than you would have me say. Keep me on the path that you have laid out for me today, and show me satan's tactics in advance.

I acknowledge the whole armor of God. I pray that every thought that satan or any of his kingdom tries to put in my mind will bounce off the helmet of salvation and return to the sender. Heal every memory that could hold me back from being all that you want me to be. I recognize that I have on the breastplate of righteousness, my loins are girded with the truth, and my feet are shod with the preparation of the gospel of peace. I take up the sword of the spirit, and the shield of faith.

Now, for myself and all the people I am going to refer to, I ask you to draw us to yourself, convict us mightily of our sins, keep us from temptation, deliver us from evil and cover us with the blood of Jesus. Dispatch angels (and I now dispatch them) to keep us from any kind of accidents, harm, injuries, illness, death, destruction, disease, pain or infection.

Bind our marriages together and make us one in you. Bind our families together and make us one in you. If there is anyone in our lives that you do not approve of, I ask you to move them out and move in the people that you do approve of. Bless every bite of food we eat, and the air we breathe, or any medication we take, and let it help us and not hurt us. Bless our finances and give us as much as we can handle without sinning against you.

Now, satan, I come against you and your entire kingdom and I declare, in the Name of Jesus, that you cannot and will not have any part of my life or the lives of the people I refer to, in any way, shape or form. You can have nothing to do with our minds, bodies, souls, spirits, emotions and wills; our marriages, finances, friendships, acquaintances and fellowships; our homes, schools, workplaces and places of recreation; our transportation, or any vehicle that could come close to us; or any decision that is made concerning any one of us. (Now call out the name of every person that you pray for daily.)

For every person I have referred to, I now break every curse, spell, and hex that may have been put out against any one of us. I break the power of any curse that has come down through the inherited bloodline and every curse from a witch, warlock, or satanist; every Santerian curse, roots curse, Indian curse, voodoo curse, any curse of words spoken, or anything written or any objects. I reverse the curse and send it back to the demon that brought it in the first place, and I command that demon to go bound into uninhabited dry places in the Name of Jesus. I break every ungodly emotional soul tie that is connected to any one of us, in the Name of Jesus.

In the Name of Jesus and through His living blood, I bind and sever every cord of any prince or principality, any strong man and every spirit of darkness over my house at (your address). I put a Jesus Christ bloodline in between each one of you and I cut off your communications, confuse your camp, render you inactive, and cast you out, in Jesus' Name.

I bind and cast out every spirit of poverty, lack, confusion, cloudiness, mind binding, selfishness, anxiety, and procrastination. I bind and cast out every spirit of fear, heaviness, jealousy, bondage, whoredom, lying, perversion, slumber, and infirmity. I plead the blood of Jesus around the property line, above the roof, and below the foundation of my home, and I bind you, satan, and your entire kingdom from crossing the bloodline. I command you, for myself and the people I have just referred to, that you can have nothing to do with us or any aspect of our lives in any way, shape or form! I now call on God's warring angels to make it happen.

In the Name of Jesus, I loose myself and each family member to the power of the Holy Spirit and I speak forth blessings of prosperity, clarity, wisdom, understanding, knowledge, discernment, abundance, and good health. I also speak creativity and a sound mind. I take control of my mind and reject every evil thought and receive every good thought, in the Name of Jesus. I loose myself and my children to the ministry of the Holy Spirit and speak love, joy, peace, long-suffering, gentleness, goodness, faith, meekness, and temperance into our lives.

Satan, I take authority and command you and all your evil spirits to loose our family household and all the things you have stolen from us, including our property, income, and investments, and return it seven-fold, in Jesus' Name.

I ask you, Father, that you send your warring angels and cause to come into our family all the monies, treasure, properties, assets and things satan has stolen from us that have been ours through the blessings of Jesus Christ.

In the Name of Jesus, I take authority and bind every principality and strong man over (name business, job and any endeavors) at (name location). I come against and cast out every spirit of fear, mismanagement, poverty, confusion, lack, failure and bankruptcy. In the Name of Jesus and through the power of the Holy Spirit, I loose sound management, prosperity, clarity, wisdom, knowledge, blessings, profit, honesty, success, and favor from any business associates. Father, I ask you, in the Name of Jesus, that you send warring angels to go before me to accomplish these blessings and create favor in my business.

In the Name of Jesus Christ and through His living blood, I bind you, satan, and your entire kingdom so that you cannot and will not be active in (your county) in any person or animal. I come against your strongholds over every place dealing in drugs, pornography, prostitution, bars and nude bars, places selling witchcraft paraphernalia, palm readers, and any place worshiping a false god. Through the power of the Holy Spirit vested in me, I tear down and curse these businesses at the roots and command them to dry up and go away.

Lord, don't let me be just a warrior in your kingdom, but let me be a mighty warrior and a frontline soldier, so that when I see you face to face, you will say, "Well done, good and faithful servant; come on in." Amen.

There are many scriptures that tell us how we should pray, but no one needs to do a study on prayer to know this basic fact: If you love someone, you will talk to him. We all need to realize and remember that our heavenly Father loves us. The Bible is full of references to His love for us and the most obvious sign of His love is His Son's death on the cross for our sins.

This kind of love deserves our love, respect, honor and worship! We need to be talking to the Lord continually and not just when we have needs. We should tell Him how wonderful He is and how much we appreciate His goodness and mercy toward us.

Pray without ceasing. (I Thess. 5:17)

Without ceasing means continual, unending, perpetual, immeasurable, infinite, limitless. If we were totally honest about how much time we spend in prayer (loving communication) with God, we would all FALL SHORT of what God deserves in return for His love for us!

The following is a good evening prayer for ending your day.

EVENING WARFARE PRAYER

Begin with praise and thanksgiving, then continue.

Father, I ask you, in the Name of Jesus, to dispatch (and I now dispatch them with my mouth) mighty warring angels right now to hold back the forces of satan and his kingdom while I sleep.

Satan, you and any evil spirit in your kingdom that could be in or around our properties, I bind you and drive you out in the Name of Jesus. Any astral projection or soul travel spirits that could be in or around our property, I command you, in the Name of Jesus, to go back where you came from.

I cover my mind, brain and memories, my conscious, unconscious and subconscious, with the blood of Jesus. I bind up any spirits of terror, fear, nightmares, or torment with the blood of Jesus.

Lord Jesus, protect our property, vehicles, families (wherever they are), and our pastor. Give us supernaturally good rest, speak to us through our dreams, and let us awaken refreshed.

I cover our home above, below, and on all sides with the blood of Jesus. I also cover our automobiles, and speak peace upon us all. In Jesus' Name. Amen.

I have called upon thee, for thou wilt hear me, O God: incline thine ear unto me, and hear my speech. Shew thy marvellous lovingkindness, O thou that savest by thy right hand them which put their trust in thee from those that rise up against them. Keep me as the apple of the eye, hide me under the shadow of thy wings. (Ps. 17:6-8) Amen.

10

Explaining Your Homework Assignment

Explaining Your Homework Assignment

This is an instructional book and we want to lead you into workable methods so you will understand and be able to implement deliverance in your own life. Hence, we are including some homework for you personally. Please do not just read over this portion, but *do the assignments.* You will be glad you did!

OPEN DOOR LIST

The demonic kingdom may have gained access into your life through people and activities that are outlined in the eight specific categories listed on the following page. Make your own list in private.

When we counsel, we do not get involved in the details of a person's past, because it is not necessary. There are areas of a person's life that are between the individual and God alone. Because that is our policy and our ministry is not intimidating in any way, we have many well-known personalities and pastors coming to us for deliverance.

If you are a born-again child of God, satan and his kingdom have no legal right to you and cannot enter your life unless:

1. You allow it.
2. The enemy has gained a legal entry from your past through your inherited bloodline
3. You have opened a door to satan through sin in your life.

Somehow a bridge has been created from satan to you and you are now being prepared to burn that bridge, closing the entry door forever! This can only be accomplished through prayer. If you begin to write down names haphazardly on a piece of paper, this exercise will not work. God knows when a satanic influence entered your life and He will show you, so that you can be effective in making your list.

Most demonic influences enter during childhood, because satan does not play fair. He preys on little children! You may have forgotten some things from your childhood, or deem them insignificant, but they could be the key that opens a big door in your being able to be SET FREE. Spend time in prayer, and the Holy Spirit will show you what you need to bring to remembrance, because He wants you free more than even you want to be free.

EIGHT OPEN DOOR CATEGORIES

1. Unforgiveness/Judgments
2. Occult Activities
3. Sexual Sin Outside Of Marriage
4. Ungodly Soul Ties
5. Broken Covenants/Vows
6. Pride
7. Idolatry
8. Any Unconfessed Sin

1. UNFORGIVENESS/JUDGMENTS

On a separate sheet of paper, make a list of anyone in your past that you have had any unforgiveness toward. Even though we know that everything was covered at Calvary, and you forgave everyone and God forgave you, all of that was accomplished in the "spirit" man. We are now referring to your "soulish" man. Even though your spirit man is covered and sealed by the Holy Spirit because you are born again, and the devil can't touch you, he does have access to and can influence your "soulish" man. This consists of your MIND (memories), your EMOTIONS (how you feel about people and things), and your WILL (what you want).

Satan has access to the "soulish" part of us and that is where we all have problems. He knows all our memories because, after all, he was there. Never forget that satan and his kingdom have only three assignments: to KILL, STEAL and DESTROY.

The thief cometh not, but for to steal, and to kill, and to destroy: I am come that they might have life, and that they might have it more abundantly. (John 10:10)

Satan and his kingdom do not sleep, so remember that they are on duty twenty-four hours a day, doing their dirty work. Christians are their target, because satan already has control of all who haven't accepted Christ as their personal Savior.

Even though you have forgiven everyone in the spirit realm, you can still be tormented by the devil in your "soulish" area because there are lingering hurts, fears, anger, lust, rejection and other things in your background which were there before you were born again. Demons can bring up memories and emotions on a constant basis in an effort to defeat you and hold you back from becoming all that God wants you to be. This is the reason it is helpful to list each person you have not forgiven.

To help you compile your own list, we are offering some examples of situations that might have happened:

1. Boyfriend/girlfriend who jilted you for someone else.
2. Parent who punished you unjustly.
3. Parent who favored a brother/sister over you.
4. School teacher who embarrassed you in front of the class.
5. Someone who molested you or your children.
6. Someone who stole your money and did not return it.
7. Person who abandoned you.
8. Person who lied to you.
9. Someone who got the promotion you deserved.
10. Someone who caused the death of a person you loved.
11. Your own name (you may need to forgive yourself).
12. Someone who borrowed money and never repaid it.

Following are some true examples of the things that were revealed when people prayed and asked God to show them who to put on their "unforgiveness" list.

ACCOUNT

Gregory was a burly man who spoke with a marked New York accent. He told us that he was driving to work the day after we had instructed him to make his "unforgiveness" list when he heard these words in his mind, "You need to forgive those two girls." He asked, "What girls, Lord? What are You talking about?"

As soon as he asked that question, his mind flashed back to a scene when he was about twelve years old. He was walking to a swimming pool in Long Island with his swimsuit wrapped up in a towel under his arm. Suddenly he met two beautiful young girls about fourteen years of age. He had just entered puberty and was beginning to get hair on his body. His legs were covered with hair but his chest was still totally bare. As he approached the girls, his heart began pounding because he got nervous as he noticed how gorgeous they were. As he passed the girls on the sidewalk, one of them looked at him and said, "Hey, kid, you need to take some of that hair off your legs and put it on your chest!" Then they laughed at him.

Gregory had completely forgotten that episode but it must have been very important to him for the Lord to "pull back the curtain" and reveal it to him. Probably that was the opening in his life for feelings of rejection, shyness, and insecurity to enter. So, years later, even though he never knew the names of the girls, he put them on his list of people he needed to forgive.

When we met him, Gregory was a mature man of the Word and taught the Bible, but he still fought feelings of inadequacy. After his deliverance, he turned into someone with the boldness of Elijah. Why? Because satan no longer had him bound in his emotions.

ACCOUNT—Move the Bed

For as long as she could remember, Wilda Sue, a woman in her forties, had not been able to sleep in a bed that was in the corner of the room. If she was a guest in someone's home and was asked to sleep in a corner bed, she would pull it out from the wall, sleep in it, then push it back into the corner the next morning.

She never knew why she felt this way nor could she remember anything in her past that would account for these feelings. Oddly, however, she could remember nothing that happened in her life before the age of seven. This is highly unusual. After we explained the list on unforgiveness to her, she was willing and even eager to pray and hear from God about what names to write on her list.

Wilda Sue was a precious, devoted Christian who loved the Lord with all her heart. She raised her children to love Him, and her life was a witness of God's love. She was kind and giving, and was always doing nice things for people.

She told us that after she prayed about her list, the Lord opened her memories to a scene that she had completely forgotten. She saw herself at the age of three crumpled in a fetal position on a bed IN THE CORNER OF THE ROOM and her father was beating her unmercifully with a belt. These beatings must have opened up doors in her life that allowed spirits of fear, rejection, hate, revenge and much, much more to enter

Wilda Sue told us that she put her father's name on her list and after the deliverance session, she was never again plagued with the fear of sleeping on a bed in the corner of the room. As long as satan kept that memory hidden from her, he could keep her in bondage (in the "soulish" area of her emotions/feelings). However, when she remembered and forgave her father, the bridge that the demonic kingdom has used to enter her life was totally destroyed!

We read in Matthew 18:34 and 35 that satan has a legal right to torment you twenty-four hours a day if you have unforgiveness in your heart. He can make you sleep too much or he can make you sleepless. He can TORMENT, TORMENT, TORMENT you! Satan knows the Word of God better than we do; after all, he was around when it was written.

And his lord was wroth, and delivered him to the tormentors, till he should pay all that was due unto him. So likewise shall my heavenly Father do also unto you, if ye from your hearts forgive not every one his brother their trespasses. (Matt. 18:34, 35)

JUDGMENTS

We also need to release judgments that we have against people. The following accounts will show you the outcome of releasing judgments.

ACCOUNT—You Forgave the Man But You Didn't Forgive the Debt

Julie heard this sentence come into her mind during a Sunday evening church service. There was a strong anointing in the service and she knew God was speaking—and she also knew exactly what it meant. Her former husband had not paid child support for years and arrearage had mounted to approximately $35,000. She had developed a judgment in her mind about him that wasn't very good.

Julie loved God and was living a victorious Christian life. She had forgiven her ex-husband—but, without realizing it, she continued to *judge* him. She would make remarks like, "At least he could work at McDonald's and make some money." She was constantly calling to see if he had paid any support money into the state depository.

After hearing from God and obeying Him, she went to her ex-husband and told him that she was releasing him from all past, present and future child support. When she did that, something broke in the spirit realm. He began to weep, and said, "You know, this is like getting born again. You get something you don't even deserve." About two weeks later, he called her and told her that because of what she had done, he had come back to the Lord and was serving Him.

Whenever you have a judgment against a person, you hold that person in prison. God wants you to release it. The result will be that not only will the other person be free—but you will, too! Julie no longer has to think about her ex-husband or the money, because that part is over.

Julie's ex-husband began to take pride in himself, and improved his appearance. Before, he had been unhappy with himself, was bound by alcohol, and could not get a job. But God turned all that around.

This example is not meant to imply that every woman should release an ex-spouse from his obligation to support the children. But in this particular case, Julie heard from God and the lives of her ex-husband, her children, and herself all became free because God knows everything—and He knows what is best!

ACCOUNT—Bad Dad

Kirk was living on the streets when he ventured into a church service that Sunday morning several years ago. Paul ministered to him at the altar and could smell alcohol on his breath.

Kirk was extremely handsome. Tall with blond hair and blue eyes, he had the physique of a man who spent lots of time in the gym. His suntan was so deep that he could have been mistaken for a lifeguard.

He said to Paul, "If you can't help me, I'm going to kill myself. I actually tried to kill myself last week, but I failed both times. You're my only hope! I'm a hopeless alcoholic and I've been through every program that Tampa has to offer. I paid someone $400 to hypnotize me—and even that didn't work! I've been an alcoholic for fifteen years and it's hopeless! I have lost my job, my family and my home. So now I have no desire to live."

Paul scheduled Kirk for a counseling appointment the very next day and we explained everything to him. We gave him the **Open Door List** to fill out and had him come back the following day for deliverance.

When Kirk arrived the next day, Paul asked him if he had forgiven everyone, as we had shown him to do. "Yes, I have forgiven everyone except my father—and *I hate him*! I cannot remember one good day growing up because of him. He abused my mother and me every day of our lives. My life is destroyed because of him."

Paul replied, "Well, the Bible tells us to forgive and you can choose to forgive him with your free will. You see, Kirk, you can't trust your feelings, because they are part of your *soulish* area and satan has access to your feelings." Then Paul opened the Word and read the following:

For if ye forgive men their trespasses, your heavenly father will also forgive you: but if ye forgive not men their trespasses, neither will your Father forgive your trespasses. (Matt. 6:14, 15)

"Kirk, will you choose to trust the Word of God more than you trust your feelings?" Kirk agreed that he wanted to trust God and forgive his father.

Next, Paul asked him to release the judgment he had against his father and instructed Kirk to repeat after him: "I release the judgment against my father!" Kirk tried to speak but he could only choke, so Paul repeated the phrase. Again Kirk tried to speak but nothing came out. A third time Kirk tried but was unable to speak. Finally Paul blurted out, "You evil spirit that is binding his tongue, I command you in the Name of Jesus to loose him!" and immediately Kirk screamed out, "I RELEASE THE JUDGMENT AGAINST MY FATHER!" Suddenly, with no warning, he vomited.

When Kirk finally settled down, he was quiet for a moment, then he jumped up and started dancing and hopping around the room, shouting the praises of the Lord. We saw him smiling for the first time, a great, wide grin from ear to ear. A glorious sight.

We kept in close contact with Kirk and we know he never took another drink. He got a job and an apartment, and was given permission to see his son again.

About six months after Kirk's deliverance, his mother died suddenly. She has watching his son in his apartment while Kirk was working and she accidentally fell, hitting her head on the corner of a table. As a result of the injury she died two days later. Even during this sad, stressful time, Kirk did not take a drink. This was a perfect time for satan to tempt him to drink, but the demon of bondage to drink was gone and Kirk was free.

2. OCCULT (list these on a separate sheet)

List all occult activities in which you have ever been involved. Following are some examples:

- Ouija board
- Astral projection
- Meditation
- Water witching
- Superstition
- Palm reading
- New Age
- Witchcraft
- Satanism
- Hypnotism
- False religions
- Tarot cards
- Psychics

Going to a source other than God for spiritual information is of the occult. Demons are waiting in line for a human to call them up and they will be in your midst in a split second. They cannot do their dirty work without a body to inhabit, so they want you to open yourself up and invite them in through occult activities. The good news is that there are a host of God's angels standing at attention with their swords drawn just waiting for you to dispatch them into a situation. And remember! *There are two good angels for every bad one!*

3. SEXUAL SINS

On a separate sheet of paper, list every person that you have had a sexual relationship with outside of marriage. If you cannot remember names, just list situations and approximate times. Whenever there is a sexual union or sexual activity of any kind (outside of the marriage vows), demons have a legal right to flow from one person to another.

Satan and his kingdom realize that they have a legal right to enter a person whenever they transgress the laws of God. I believe that is why he is causing the world to believe that sex is acceptable outside of marriage. It gives him free rein to enter humans and destroy their lives. Satan is using television, billboards, magazines, videos, and many other things to blind people into believing that they can be sexually active and get by with it. Transgressing God's law is far more deadly than the AIDS virus.

If you commit this list to prayer, God will show you what you need to write down. Here are some examples:

- Sexual partners (outside of marriage)
- Anyone who molested/raped you
- Sexual intercourse with an animal

ACCOUNT—Grand Mal Seizure

Molly and her husband were grandparents and had been pillars of the church for years. She had served as a Sunday school teacher and he was a deacon. They had even spent several years as missionaries after they graduated from Bible college. Molly was attending a deliverance seminar when a word of knowledge came forth saying that someone in the audience had committed a sexual sin a certain number of years before and God wanted to set them free.

Molly ran to the front of the auditorium, and cried, "It was me. I did commit sexual sin at that time but it was with my husband. We had sexual relations before we married, even though we were engaged." At that time an *ungodly soul tie* was broken between her and her husband and a spirit of darkness was commanded to leave. Molly immediately fell to the floor and suffered a grand mal epileptic seizure. After only a couple of minutes, she jumped up from the floor and shouted, "I'm healed! I'm healed!"

She testified that she had never had a seizure before her marriage. After she was married, she had mild seizures, but they only happened occasionally, at first. Then they increased in frequency until she was taking the maximum doses of medication and was still having two seizures per month. After a seizure, she would have to go into a dark room and stay for at least two full days before she could come out. The significance of sharing that point was that she had just had a seizure, but she was immediately fine when it passed. As that demon left her body, it left in the form of a seizure and a year later she wrote that she had never again had a seizure.

It is important to note that no one in Molly's family suffered from seizures, so there was no family history whatsoever. However, with one word of knowledge from the Throne of God, Molly was set free of the spirit of infirmity that had entered her body through that ungodly sexual relationship.

ACCOUNT—Transfer of Demons

We ministered to a witch who told us that before she became a Christian, she had been extremely active sexually, and she would put fifteen to twenty demons in every man she had sex with. She was able to do this because she knew she had a legal right to do so—and because she enjoyed it! Now she feels bad about what she did. She commented to us that those men went home with a lot more than they bargained for.

4. UNGODLY SOUL TIES (list these on a separate sheet)

Ungodly soul ties are developed whenever the spiritual boundaries set up by God are violated, such as when the marriage bed becomes defiled, or through fornication, adultery, evil friendships, unnatural and perverted family relationships and incest.

Satan knows that he cannot get to you without using someone close to you; that is why your biggest battle may be a family member. If a stranger came up to you and told you he hated you, what would it matter to you? You wouldn't care; you would just shrug it off and go about your business. But if your spouse or mother or child told you they hated you, that would probably feel like someone stuck a knife into your heart.

Satan is not stupid; he knows exactly how to get to you. He knows which relative or friend to use to say something to hurt you, make you feel angry, or rejected. He can even cause them to give you certain looks to cause you to have those feelings. Here is a list of examples of those with whom ungodly soul ties can be developed:

- Parents (step or adoptive)
- Brothers and sisters (half/step/adopted)
- Any sexual partner outside of marriage
- Any aborted baby
- Any characters that you have portrayed as an actor
- Spirit guides
- Spouse/ex-spouse
- Children (step/adopted)
- Boss or person in authority over you

5. BROKEN COVENANTS AND VOWS (list these on a seprate sheet)

Broken covenants and vows can open doors in your life, because God is serious about covenants and vows. He made everlasting covenants with His people all throughout the Old Testament and He still honors covenants today. According to *Webster's Dictionary*, a covenant is, "A binding agreement made by two or more persons or parties: a formal sealed agreement or contract."

Marriage is a covenant sealed with a vow. Whether you were a believer or not when you married, if you were married before a minister or a justice of the peace, agreement to the marriage was verbally spoken. Therefore, you made a vow before God and man, and God honors vows and covenants. If you later divorce and remarry, your broken vow follows you into your new marriage. If your partner has also experienced a divorce, there are two broken vows. Sadly, these broken vows allow satan to have legal access to begin strife in your new marriage. Things will begin to go wrong, and if these broken vows are not dealt with, another divorce may result.

Broken covenants with church memberships and pledges need to be dealt with. These covenants are made to man, but also to God and, remember, God is serious about covenants.

Here are examples of covenants and vows:

- Previous marriages
- Memberships with a church
- Signing an agreement to belong to an organization
- Pledges (sometimes called "faith promises")
- Contracts to purchase

6. PRIDE (list areas of pride on a separate sheet)

What do you have in your life that makes you full of pride?

Examples:

1. Do you think you are a better mother than someone else?
2. Do you think you know more of the Bible than someone else?
3. Do you think you have a better marriage than someone else?
4. Do you think you are better in your profession than someone else?

Pride is satan's greatest tool! He fell from heaven because of it and now he wants to deceive humans to fall into that trap.

For thou hast said in thine heart, I will ascend into heaven, I will exalt my throne above the stars of God: I will sit also upon the mount of the congregation, in the sides of the north. I will ascend above the heights of the clouds; I will be like the most High. (Isaiah 14:13, 14)

7. IDOLATRY (list areas of idolatry on a separate sheet)

Thou shalt have no other gods before me. (Exodus 20:3)

The Bible speaks of the rich young ruler, whose idol was his money (Matt. 19:16-22).

What stands between you and God? What is there in your life that you would NOT be willing to give up if He asked you to?

Examples:

1. Spouse
2. Home
3. Job/position
4. Money
5. Children

8. ANY UNCONFESSED SIN (list these on a separate sheet)

We assume that people take care of any sin problem with a daily confession, but if that is not the case in your life, make sure that God has forgiven you of every sin before proceeding with deliverance.

Identify the strongholds in your life from the list in the following chapter. A problem you had in the past can still be lying dormant. Just because it is not active right now does not mean that it's gone. *Identify anything that you have ever had a problem with.* Demonic entities do not die; therefore, they are not in a hurry to do their dirty work—they have plenty of time to wait.

11

Doing Your Homework Assignment

Doing Your Homework Assignment

Now that you have thoroughly studied how to identify Stronghold Forces and how to recognize the Eight Open Door Categories, you are ready to make your own lists. Look over the lists on the following pages and remember, a problem you had in the past can still be lying dormant. *Identify anything that you have ever had a problem with.* After you make your lists, you will be able to burn the bridge between you and satan, closing the entry door forever!

STRONGHOLD FORCES

HAUGHTY (Proverbs 16:18)
Pride • Perfection • Accusation • Competition • Mockery • Stubbornness • Self-righteous • Gossip • Boastful

DEAF AND DUMB (Mark 9:17-29)
Mental Illness • Insanity • Seizures/Epilepsy • Double-mindedness • Suicidal • Multi-personality • Hyperactivity • Self-mutilation

SLUMBER (Romans 11:8)
Withdrawal • Mind binding • Sleepiness • Forgetfulness • Stupidity • Daydreaming • Trances • Inactivity • Lethargy • Sluggishness

FAMILIAR (I Samuel 28:7)
Necromancer • Clairvoyant • Spirit guides • CURSES: Inherited, Witch or warlock, Indian, Santeria, Roots, Voodoo • Words that have been spoken

DIVINATION (Acts 16:16-18)
Soothsayer • Fortune telling • Horoscope • Stargazer/Zodiac • Occult • Witch/Warlock • Magic (white or black) • Seances

FEAR (II Timothy 1:7)

Insecurity • Inadequacy • Inferiority complex • Timidity • Worry • Fear of authority • Sensitivity • Terror • Torment/horror • Nightmares • Phobias (dark, heights, future) • Anxiety • Nervous • Abandonment

HEAVINESS (Isaiah 61:3)

Rejection • Despair • Grief • Fatigue • Guilt • Self-pity • Loneliness • Depression • Manic depression • Gloominess/sadness • Insomnia

JEALOUSY (Numbers 5: 11-14)

Impatience • Bitterness • Strife • Covetousness • Control (Jezebel) • Revenge/Retaliation • Suspicion • Anger/Rage • Hatred • Wrath • Murder • Violence • Restlessness • Selfishness

LYING (II Chron. 18:22)

Deception/Lies • Exaggeration • Profanity • Hypocrisy • Condemning others • Theft • Isolation • Vanity

ANTI-CHRIST (I John 4:3)

Doubt and unbelief • Rebellion • Witchcraft • Self-exaltation

POVERTY (John 10:10)

BONDAGE (Romans 8:15)

Hindering (can't call on God) (hold back God's call on your life) • Greed • Gluttony • Obesity • Addiction (drugs, alcohol, nicotine) • Bulimia • Anorexia • Poverty

INFIRMITY (Luke 13:11)

Inherited curse (infirmity) • Arthritis • Asthma/hay fever/allergies • Fever • Cancer • Death • Every disease • Pain

WHOREDOM (Hosea 4:12)

Prostitution • Cults • Religious • Legalism • Idolatry (money, etc.) • Emotional Weakness • Fornication • Adultery

PERVERSION (Isaiah 19:14)

Word twisting • Lust • Lesbianism • Homosexuality • Masturbation • Sodomy • Bestiality • Child molestation • Exhibitionism • Pornography • Seducing spirit

II
OPEN DOOR LIST

1. **UNFORGIVENESS**: List all people from childhood to the present (dead or alive) for whom you now have or have ever had any unforgiveness or resentment.

2. OCCULT: List all dealings you have had with the occult (Ouija boards, seances, horoscopes, New Age, superstition, witchcraft, oaths, Santeria, palm reader, roots, others).

3. SEXUAL SIN: List all people you have been sexually involved with outside of marriage (rape, molestation, incest, homosexuality, lesbianism, bestiality, even your spouse if you came together sexually prior to marriage).

4. SOUL TIES: List all people (dead or alive) that have had an ungodly control over you. Also, your mother, father, stepparents, spouse(s), grandparents, boss, spirit guides, abortions, hypnotist, ex-spouse(s), brothers/sisters (step or half), children (step, adopted, foster) and any others. Also include the names of anybody from #3 above (sexual partners).

5. COVENANTS, VOWS: List all broken covenants and vows of the past (marriages, church membership, contracts).

6. PRIDE: List things in your life that you are prideful about (better mother, better marriage, better profession).

7. IDOLATRY: List things that you would not be willing to give up for God.

8. UNCONFESSED SIN: List any sin you have not already asked forgiveness for.

III
PROCLAMATIONS

Salvation is a prerequisite. There is absolutely no sense praying deliverance or any proclamation prayers unless you are born again. We do not pray deliverance for anyone unless we know they are Christians (or choose to become one before we pray). You see, it is one thing to get free, but it is another thing to STAY FREE. And a person will not be able to stay free unless he has the power of the Holy Spirit in him. The Holy Spirit comes in when a person is born again.

If you have never heard what we call "the plan of salvation," please read the following verses. If you then believe in your heart, you can pray and ask Jesus to become your Lord and Savior.

You might say, "But I am not a bad person; I go to church and do the best I can." That could very well be true, but look at what the Bible says abut the condition of the unsaved man.

As it is written, There is none righteous, no, not one. (Rom. 3:10)

For all have sinned, and come short of the glory of God. (Rom. 3:23)

Because Adam sinned, we are all born with a sin nature.

For the wages of sin is death; but the gift of God is eternal life through Jesus Christ our Lord. (Rom. 6:23)

We deserve to pay for our sins, but God loved us so much that He gave His precious Son, Jesus Christ, to die on Calvary for our sins. By His shed blood, our sins are washed as white as snow.

For God so loved the world, that he gave his only begotten Son, that whosoever believeth in him should not perish, but have everlasting life. (John 3:16)

But God commendeth his love toward us, in that, while we were yet sinners, Christ died for us. (Rom. 5:8)

What can we do about this gift of salvation and Jesus dying on the cross for our sins? What must we do to be saved?

That if thou shalt confess with thy mouth the Lord Jesus, and shalt believe in thine heart that God hath raised him from the dead, thou shalt be saved. For with the heart man believeth unto righteousness; and with the mouth confession is made unto salvation. (Rom. 10:9, 10)

For whosoever shall call upon the name of the Lord shall be saved. (Rom. 10:13)

If you want to make a decision to believe in Jesus Christ and ask Him to be your Savior, PRAY THIS PRAYER:

> *Heavenly Father, I ask you to forgive me for my sins and anything I have ever done to offend you.*
>
> *I believe that Jesus is your only begotten Son, and that He died for my sins.*
>
> *Please come into my heart and be lord of my life.*
>
> *In Jesus' Name. Amen.*

Now you are ready to proceed with the Prayers of Proclamation.

PROCLAMATION OF FORGIVENESS

Lord, I want to confess that I have not loved, but have resented certain people and have unforgiveness in my heart. Lord, I call upon you to help me forgive. Now I *choose* to forgive with my free will, and release all judgments against (at this time read aloud the names of everyone on your **Open Door List**). Now I forgive and accept myself, in the Name of Jesus.

PROCLAMATION FOR OCCULT CONFESSION

Lord Jesus, I confess seeking from satan and his kingdom the help that should have come from God Almighty. I confess as sin (at this point name all occult sins from your **Open Door List**) and even those I do not remember. Lord, I repent and renounce these sins and ask you to forgive me. In the Name of Jesus I now close the door to all occult practices. Satan, I rebuke you, in the Name of Jesus, and I command all spirits to leave me now.

PROCLAMATION TO BE SET FREE FROM SEXUAL SIN

Thank you, Jesus, for dying on the cross that I might be forgiven. I confess all my sexual sin and invite you, Jesus, to be lord of my life, especially my sexuality. I ask you to set me free from everyone I have had sexual relations with outside of marriage. I recognize that this is sin and I do not want to continue these relationships. (Name each relationship aloud from your **Open Door List**.)

Any spirit in satan's kingdom that has come into me through these sexual relationships, I use the authority I have in Jesus Christ, that you have no further right in my spirit, soul, and body, and I order you to leave me now, in the Name of Jesus.

PROCLAMATION BREAKING UNGODLY SOUL TIES

Thank you, Jesus, for dying that I might be set free. I invite you, Lord Jesus, to be lord of my life, and I ask you to set me free. I confess and repent of my sin. I forgive and loose in the freedom of my forgiveness those with whom I have ungodly soul ties. I now renounce any ungodly soul ties with (name aloud every person[s] on the **Open Door List** of soul ties and repeat the name[s] from the sexual sin list). I now use the authority I have in Jesus Christ and break and renounce these ungodly soul ties and command all demonic spirits that entered me through these relationships to leave me now.

PROCLAMATION ON BROKEN COVENANTS/VOWS

Lord Jesus, I confess that I have broken covenants/vows. I recognize this is sin and I ask you, Lord Jesus, to forgive me now for breaking these covenants between me and (name each relationship aloud: marriage, church membership, pledges, and contracts). I now use my authority in Jesus Christ to break any curses that this has brought upon me and order every spirit in satan's kingdom to leave me now.

PROCLAMATION TO BE SET FREE FROM PRIDE

Lord Jesus, I recognize that I have felt prideful about (name each thing you have written down on your paper) and I ask you to forgive me now. I know that anything I have ever done of any worth has come from you, and I am sorry that I have gotten "puffed up" thinking that it was "me" that accomplished these things and not you. I humble myself and pray that you will cause me always to exercise humility.

PROCLAMATION ON IDOLATRY

Father, I realize that anything that is in my life that I have put first and ahead of you is idolatry. I confess that I have put (name each thing on your list) before you in my life and I repent and ask your forgiveness. I want you to be first in my life.

PROCLAMATION OF ANY
UNCONFESSED SIN

> Heavenly Father, I realize that what I have done is sin. Please forgive (list everything you have written down on your **Open Door List** as unconfessed sin). Wash me clean in the Name of Jesus and fill me with your Holy Spirit. I want to be pure and holy and acceptable in your sight.

You have just BURNED THE BRIDGE (in the spirit realm). Now you need to do it in the physical realm by burning the "list of names (**Open Door List**)" that had you bound!

You have now closed the doors and satan and his kingdom no longer have a legal right in your life. He is trespassing on God's property!

Doing the assignments won't set you free but you are now ready for the deliverance prayer. Pray for yourself and if you do not feel comfortable with this, get together with a Christian friend, a prayer partner, a pastor, or someone else to pray with you. We recommend that two, possibly three, pray deliverance together.

Begin with the haughty spirit on your **Stronghold List** and then call out every spirit identified on the list. Continue until you have covered them all, including perversion.

You will begin to experience feelings of freedom like never before, and God's presence will fill your life. Now you are beginning to "climb the mountain of holiness."

And now you are ready to TAKE THE WAR TO THE ENEMY!

12

Climbing the Mountain of Holiness

Climbing the Mountain of Holiness

OBEDIENCE BRINGS HOLINESS

Thy word have I hid in mine heart, that I might not sin against thee. (Ps. 119:11)

But if we walk in the light, as he is in the light, we have fellowship one with another, and the blood of Jesus Christ his Son cleanseth us from all sin. (I John 1:7)

And Samuel said, Hath the Lord as great delight in burnt offerings and sacrifices as in obeying the voice of the Lord? Behold, to obey is better than sacrifice, and to hearken than the fat of rams. (I Samuel 15:22)

God is looking for our obedience—not our sacrifices. You may be sacrificing hours to serve in a certain ministry or even to spend time in prayer. More important than any of that, however, is your total obedience! There must not be anything in your life between you and God. Not your marriage, your work, your recreation, or your ministry. God wants your total commitment.

God also wants every oppression out of your life, everything that will hold you back from your relationship with Him. He wants everything in the flesh to die so His light can shine through you. Deal with things such as:

- unforgiveness
- judgment
- jealousy
- bitterness
- bondage
- fear
- rejection
- depression

As these and other things are removed from your life, God's light begins to shine through you. His light brings one to a higher level and we must have the light of God to walk in His authority.

GOD'S LIGHT

O house of Jacob, come ye, and let us walk in the light of the Lord. (Isaiah 2:5)

Ye are the light of the world. A city that is set on an hill cannot be hid. (Matt. 5:14)

His light in us shows our true condition, our impurities. Jesus is coming for a church without "spot or wrinkle" and He wants us to deal with all the impurities. Only as we deal with these impurities will we begin to know His heart. He wants to trust us with His knowledge, and He can do this only to the degree that we know His heart.

When God begins to release His gifts in us, His power goes to work in our lives. Therefore, He is looking for those He can trust with His power and grace. He wants to release more power now than at any other time in history. We are a special generation. See Acts 2:17.

How can we prepare ourselves to receive His power? By daily taking up His cross and laying ourselves on the altar. By dealing with our revealed impurities, we draw closer to Jesus. He said, *If you seek Me, you will find Me.* We see here that *we* determine how close we get to Jesus, not the other way around. If we draw near to Him, He will draw near to us. The more we seek Him, the more mature we become; the more mature we become, the more we realize our desperate need of Him. Likewise, the more we walk in the light, the more we seek to be exposed and more of God's power is revealed through us.

GOD'S POWER

We seek God's power for one purpose: to see lives changed. We see the sick healed, miracles performed, and people set free from bondage.

Even when His power works through us, we cannot fully comprehend the power of His Word. God has ALL POWER; His Word is power! And the power of His Word will restore all the dead who ever lived. He upholds all things by the power of His Word, so nothing is a strain for Him. All creation exists because of His Word and is held together by His Word. Think about it! God's power is awesome! And He wants the power of His Word to work through us—but this can happen only to the measure that He can trust us.

We will be judged by the words we speak, so we must use wisdom! Those who are careless with words cannot be trusted with the power of His Word. When God entrusts us with His Word, He is entrusting us with the power that holds the universe together. Think of it! A single word from God is more valuable than any force on earth. And God says that He is going to release a greater portion of His power in these last days than ever before in history—to those He can trust.

CAUTION! There is great danger in walking in His great power. There can be delusion if we think God's power in our lives is His endorsement of our message. We must be like Paul: Learn to glory in our weakness more than our strength. When we look at ourselves, pride can set in and we will begin to fall. That is what happened to satan. *Pride goeth before destruction and a haughty spirit before a fall.*

All we need is faith in Jesus and love for Him. We must always realize that Jesus in us is light and that is what gives us power to do His work through His Word.

GOD'S LOVE

God demonstrates His power because He wants His people to love and obey Him, not because of fear. Perfect love casts out fear.

We must have the love of Jesus, or His power in us will corrupt us. Our goal in seeking Him must be love, not power, because faith works by love.

This is my commandment, That ye love one another, as I have loved you. (John 15:12)

Love is a fruit of the Spirit.

And we have known and believed the love that God hath to us. God is love; and he that dwelleth in love dwelleth in God, and God in him. (1 John 4:16)

- Perfect love brings holiness and righteousness.
- Love is the greatest weapon to destroy satan's kingdom.
- Love never fails.
- Love will build God's kingdom.
- Love is the banner over God's army.

The light of Jesus will expose all impurities and your willingness to deal with each one brings more light into your life. The more *light*, the more *love*. The more continued *light*, the more continued *love*. The more *love*, the more *power*. The more continued *love*, the more continued *power*.

Climb the mountain of holiness and let God show off in your life. God is love!

And he said unto them, I beheld Satan as
lightning fall from heaven.

Behold, I give unto you power to tread
on serpents and scorpions,
and over all the power of the enemy:
and nothing shall by any means hurt you.

Notwithstanding in this rejoice not,
that the spirits are subject unto you;
but rather rejoice, because
your names are written in heaven.

Luke 10:18-20

Paul and Claire Hollis minister nationally and have seen thousands of people freed from demonic influence. They each hold a degree of Ph.D. in Clinical Christian Psychology, and conduct private and group counseling sessions. They also conduct seminars and teach a School of Deliverance. They have been featured speakers and guests on television talk shows across America.

Other books by Paul and Claire

DEMON SLAYERS Actual case histories of people who have gone through deliverance. Relive the experiences with them as this book takes you through shocking, extreme, intense battles of Good versus Evil—and Good *always* prevails!

THE LIGHT Go on an adventure with JJ and Lynn as they visit a mysterious town. The curtain gets pulled back on some fascinating, supernatural things that have been covered over for years. JJ and Lynn get into trouble and find themselves in life-threatening situations. Get to know Lana, who states, "I hate those two! Our leader hates them, too. And his number-one goal is to completely destroy them!"

DELAYED INVASION A U.S. military crew in Germany mysteriously intercepts a plot by demon entities to overthrow the governments of the world by disguising themselves as beings from outer space. Go with JJ and Lynn as they visit Washington, DC and get caught up in the middle of the invasion plans.

DECEIVED Worldwide revival is taking place on planet Earth and people everywhere are uniting, with Christ as the common denominator. Satan and Lana have devised a plan that cannot fail! Satan tells Lana, "I want you to pick out two men, one in the political field and the other in religion. Set them up as world leaders, then, when the time is right, I will enter one of them just like I did Judas Iscariot. Then I WILL RULE THE WORLD!" Even as unseen entities take over the world, the majority of people are unaware of what is going on.

If these books are not yet available in your local bookstore, order them direct by e-mail, calling, or faxing our Tampa office.

Warfare Plus Ministries offers many tape series on special demonic warfare issues and mini-books on individual stronghold forces. For a listing of our ministry tapes, manuals and other material, visit our web site or write to us. You may also request a product order form at the same address.

If you are interested in attending a group seminar or want to schedule a group seminar in your local church, please call or write to us:

Paul and Claire Hollis
Warfare Plus Ministries, Inc.
PMB #206
4577 Gunn Highway
Tampa, FL 33624 USA
(813) 265-2379
Fax : (813) 908-0228
E-mail: WarfareP@aol.com
Web Site: www.warfareplus.com